AN IMPOSSIBLE MATCH

The Hasting Sisters
Book Three

Sandra Sookoo

Dragonblade Publishing, Inc. is an imprint of Kathryn Le Veque Novels, Inc.
P.O. Box 23
Moreno Valley, CA 92556
ceo@dragonbladepublishing.com

Produced in the United States of America

First Edition July 2024
Trade Paperback Edition

ARE YOU SIGNED UP FOR DRAGONBLADE'S BLOG?

You'll get the latest news and information on exclusive giveaways, exclusive excerpts, coming releases, sales, free books, cover reveals and more.

Check out our complete list of authors, too!

No spam, no junk. That's a promise!

Sign Up Here

www.dragonbladepublishing.com

Dearest Reader;

Thank you for your support of a small press. At Dragonblade Publishing, we strive to bring you the highest quality Historical Romance from some of the best authors in the business. Without your support, there is no 'us', so we sincerely hope you adore these stories and find some new favorite authors along the way.

Happy Reading!

CEO, Dragonblade Publishing

Additional Dragonblade books by Author Sandra Sookoo

The Hasting Sisters Series
The Devil's Game (Book 1)
A Second Summertime Courtship (Book 2)
An Impossible Match (Book 3)

Willful Winterbournes Series
Romancing Miss Quill (Book 1)
Pursuing Mr. Mattingly (Book 2)
Courting Lady Yeardly (Book 3)
Guarding the Widow Pellingham (Book 4)
Bedeviling Major Kenton (Book 5)
Charming Miss Standish (Book 6)
Teasing Miss Atherby (Novella)

The Storme Brother Series
The Soul of a Storme (Book 1)
The Heart of a Storme (Book 2)
The Look of a Storme (Book 3)
The Sting of a Storme (Book 4)
The Touch of a Storme (Book 5)
The Fury of a Storme (Book 6)
Much Ado About a Storme (Novella)
A Storme's First Noelle (Novella)
A Storme's Christmas Legacy (Novella)

The Lyon's Den Series
The Lyon's Puzzle
The Lyon's Redemption

Dedication

To Nicole A. I'm so glad I was fortunate enough to meet you, even if it's only been online. You are an amazing person, and I appreciate the glimmer you put into the world. Keep sparkling.

CHAPTER ONE

July 15, 1817
Landover Manor
Bedfordshire, England

"GENEVIEVE MARIE, HAVE you even heard a word that I have said?"

The annoyance in her mother's voice yanked Gigi from her delicious musings of spending this rainy, gray day in the arms of a certain young man who worked as a glass washer in one of the taverns in the village. As of yet, she'd only stolen a few kisses with him, but he was exactly the sort of man a girl could get up to scandal with.

And there had been precious little of that in her life lately.

With a little shake of her head, Gigi caught her embroidery before it slipped from her lap and then focused her gaze on her mother. Silver strands glittered in the blonde tresses, made almost magical in the candlelight. "I'm sorry, Mama. Woolgathering. Rainy days always bring out that trait." She gave her parent a little frown as she glanced around the drawing room at three of her sisters assembled there. "What did you say?"

Her mother huffed while her sisters—Cora, Anna, and Emmaline—looked on with varying expressions of amusement. "I had asked you what you planned to do with the rest of your summer. Amelia has written to me, urging me to make you find a paid position as a companion as she and Nora have done."

"Gah." Gigi briefly pointed her gaze to the ceiling. "Mia wrote to me as well, lecturing me on the same—all of her letters are the same—but that is the last thing I wish to do. It sounds dull and horrid." Her oldest sister Amelia had wed the man of her heart three months prior, a viscount with pockets to let who was a scandalous rogue and unrepentant scoundrel, but they were madly in love with each other, which was this side of sickening.

It had been Mia's idea that all the Hasting sisters take paid positions as companions to help their pay the back taxes on Landover Hall before it was taken from them, and while Mia and Cora had done just that, Gigi had held back, putting off the duty for as long as she could. That was not the path to trod that would gain her the life she wanted.

"What did you tell her?" her mother wanted to know, as she pushed and pulled her embroidery needle through the fabric.

"That I have no plans to become a companion, that being such will not give me the life I dream of, that I have far too much spirit to be subservient or docile while someone else has all the fun." Gigi shrugged. "And where did playing the part of a companion get them? Mia married a viscount with pockets near to let while Cora married a retired sea captain." Which had happened just last month. "He owns a shop in Mayfair without enough coin to do much between them, which is why she teaches piano lessons to young ladies." She was already poor; she didn't wish to continue being such. "I am done with scraping by."

"At least the girls have husbands. They aren't alone in life any longer." Her mother frowned, which only made Gigi want to do the exact opposite of what she would ask. "You would do well to find yourself settled."

"Oh, Mama, please don't lecture me on this now." She wasn't exactly jealous of her older sisters, for didn't wish to marry if it meant giving up her freedom, and honestly, she was having far too much fun jumping in and out of scandal.

"When, then? You are seven and twenty, Geneveive, and you are wasting your life by not encouraging suitors."

Across the table, Gigi's sister—and Cora's twin—moved her hands in what was sign language from the Benedictine monks. Their older sister Mia had been good on her word, and had hired a weekly tutor for Nora, so that she could learn how to talk more effectively. In fact, all the members of the Hasting family were learning it, and it seemed to give Nora peace.

"See? Even Nora thinks I shouldn't be rushed into marriage." As she spoke audibly, Gigi made a few signs to bring her sister further into the conversation. "How is it wasting one's life to *not* marry? Wouldn't it be considered irresponsible to marry someone vastly unsuited and therefore live a miserable life afterward?"

All her sisters nodded.

A sigh came from her mother. "Ordinarily, that would be a true statement. However, where you are concerned, I'm afraid it's the only way to tamp down your penchant for trouble." She laid her embroidery in her lap. "Every time a new on-dit occurs bearing your name, each instance there is a new thread of gossip swirling around you and your potential scandal, it hurts your father's heart."

Ah, so then guilt would be the motivating factor in matching her. *I don't play such games.* "Yet *he* never thought how such gossip would affect his daughters' futures when *he* chose not to pay the taxes on this pile of bricks or his other creditors." She arched one of her eyebrows. "How is what I do any different?"

"No doubt it's because you don't know the meaning of discreet," her young sister, Anna, said with a grin curving her lips.

Their parents had taken in Anna and her sister Emmaline after a fire destroyed their home and killed their mother and father.

"What is the point of engaging in scandal if no one knows about it?" Gigi couldn't help but shoot back, much to the amusement of her sisters.

Her mother, though, continued to frown. Disappointment reflected in her eyes. "Can you not see that we only want you settled and happy? I would rather you have a man to care for you once we are no longer able to do that."

"Of course I do, but I'm hoping to marry a rich man who has a title. I do not wish for a life of struggle or scrimping merely to keep a household running."

In her formative years, Gigi and her sisters had enjoyed a life of privilege. She'd even had a few Seasons in London before the family had been forced to retreat to the countryside when they could no longer afford to rent a townhouse in London. Once they were at the hall permanently and her father's financial situation had been discovered, there was no more funding for new gowns or fripperies as there was in the past. No more opportunities to go to Brighton or Bath. Various things had been sold to help raise coin, and life had generally become dull.

I don't want that for my future.

"You say you want to marry a well-to-do man, yet your behavior isn't as proper as it should be in order to attract such a gentleman." Light chastisement threaded through her mother's voice.

"What would you like of me, Mama? To sit docilely in the drawing room and embroider my life away in the hopes some man will take notice of me, and overlook the fact there is no dowry for me because Papa doesn't have a head for business?"

Tears sprang into her mother's eyes while her younger sisters gasped. "You know his mind is failing!" Truth be told, her father was upstairs resting, for he tired easily now. "Your father tried his best, but the markets were volatile from the war and the aftermath."

"Then his man-of-affairs should have guided him better. There really isn't an excuse to have nearly empty coffers at this point in his life, and with so many dependents." For that, she didn't think she could ever forgive her father. And if she were honest with herself, thinking about the future terrified her.

Her mother huffed. "Your sisters send coin home as often as they can, but they both have other responsibilities just now, and they *should* put their husbands first." Her smile didn't reach her eyes. "We shall see Amelia and Cora at Christmastide."

Before Gigi could respond, Anna jumped into the silence. "Oh, I so adore the holiday season!" Her smile was one of innocence and hope. "Perhaps one day I will marry well, for that will solve all their problems and then Gigi wouldn't need to settle for a man who doesn't truly appreciate her spirit."

"While I appreciate the support, love, you might wish to think logically." Gigi couldn't help the giggle that escaped. "Do you truly believe that some random duke or marquess is going to tumble off his horse on the road, wander up here, and then fall instantly and madly in love with you?" She snorted in derision. "Love—if it exists—doesn't happen like that. Besides, you rarely leave the house due to your scars." Which she'd obtained in the fire.

"I like to think that to the right man, none of that matters." There was a strong note of annoyance in Anna's voice as she narrowed her eyes.

"Don't give up on those dreams," Emmaline said in a quiet voice. She never left the manor because the fire had traumatized her so deeply, she now saw danger everywhere. It was probably another reason why Anna stayed near home, so that her sister wouldn't feel so alone. "If a young lady hasn't her dreams, she has nothing."

Gigi cleared her throat and took back control of the conversation. "Regardless, real life doesn't work like that. And besides, who wants the responsibility of being a duchess? There is no freedom there and far too much responsibility."

"You wouldn't enjoy that life, for there is no room to prove a sensation." Disapproval lingered in her mother's voice. "Why must you constantly chase scandal?"

"It's more entertaining and fun." Gigi shrugged. "I detest being proper as much as I detest weak-willed men, society's rules, and stays. There must be something… more out there for me than what is expected."

For a few seconds, silence brewed in the room.

Finally, her mother sighed. "You have always been my wild child."

Her youngest sister Emmaline set down her handiwork and frowned. "You are quite certain you won't be a companion like Mia and Cora? That you won't help Papa?"

Annoyance stabbed through her chest. "Perhaps someone should have the courage to ask Papa just how he let himself get into this mess, hmm?" Why should she curb her behavior when her father didn't feel the need to do the same? "Did he gamble away the contents of his coffers?" When Mia discovered how deeply his pockets were to let, she said nothing of how it happened. "Why should his daughters need to pay for his sins? The man who should have protected us all above everything?"

"You have no cause to be cruel," her mother said, then dabbed the corners of her eyes with a handkerchief.

"At times, the truth is cruel, and you shouldn't sweep such things away." When Gigi glanced at Nora, her sister encouraged her with wide eyes and a nod. Dear Nora might be mute and she might not hear correctly, but her mind was sharp. Given the opportunity, she would make a name for herself. "I won't become a companion, always at someone else's beck and call, giving up *my* position in the *beau monde* to become a glorified servant. That is *not* the life for me."

Emmaline fretted. "It's respectable work for a daughter of a family in reduced circumstances, though. I scan the newspaper every Monday for suitable positions I can take."

"Circumstances not of *my* making." In this Gigi wouldn't budge. She didn't care if it made her ungrateful. There were consequences for everyone's actions. Hadn't her parents ingrained that into her head for more years than not? "However, I *would* consider taking the position of a governess." If the children involved weren't dull. Or proper. Or whining. That would only make the days far too long.

"Oh, Gigi." Her mother sighed. "There aren't that many opportunities of said nature here in the country. It's why your sisters went to London."

"And look where it got them." Why did she feel as if she were constantly forced to defend her dreams and her own intentions because they weren't like everyone else's? "Married, one to a reformed rake and the other to a retired navy captain. Neither of whom possess a fortune, and will require my sisters to always struggle."

"But they're in love!" Anna exclaimed. "That should count for something. Isn't it the one thing everyone in the world chases?"

"Why should I become like everyone else?" More annoyed, Gigi blew out a breath. "Love sounds far too dull. I can't imagine any sort of adventure would be had once two people wed, for a woman's worth dilutes to keeping a house and becoming a mother and becoming an ornament on the arm of said man." She shook her head. "I want so much more than that."

"What do you think will happen to you if you marry a wealthy or titled man?" When Gigi didn't answer, her mother shook her head. "You are naïve yet, Genevieve, and it shows."

"No, I am hopeful and know my own mind." On this she wouldn't budge.

"However," her mother said, clearly not pleased with the interruption, "I am not quite as put out with you as I should be, because I agree with *some* of what you've said." For the space of a few heartbeats, she stared at each one of them in turn before resting her attention back on Gigi. "The girls' husbands are sweet, and they truly love your sisters. Your sisters are happy, and that is all that matters. You would do well to follow in their footsteps."

"Oh, Mama. You don't understand." Gigi harrumphed. "Love shouldn't come at the expense of being poor."

"There is more to life than bedeviling men and encouraging them to kiss you." When her sisters tittered, her mother frowned.

"Yet I will tell you this. If you are serious about taking a position as governess, the vicar in the village is in need of one for his young nieces. There are two of them. One is eight and the other is six. They've lived with him for six months, after a horrific accident took the lives of their parents as well as his."

"How fortuitous!" Anna clasped her hands. "That will keep you close. You won't go to London and fall in love, and we'll still be able to see you." Sadness filled her eyes. "While I am delighted Mia and Cora have married, I do miss them terribly."

"I understand that." For the first time during this conversation, Gigi gave thought to her sisters outside of them falling in love. "I miss them too."

She and her sisters had done everything together. They'd been her confidants, her role models, her best friends, but then they'd gone off to London. Everything had changed after that. Their attention had been readjusted. Yes, they both wrote regularly, but it wasn't the same. She would have to wait five months to see them when they came to the hall for Christmastide. And even then, she wouldn't have her sisters to herself, for they would always be concerned about the wellbeing of their husbands, and no doubt they would wish to spend time with them, for Christmastide while one was in love tended to be more magical.

Or so she'd been told by a few friends who still wrote to her.

"Since Mia and Cora went away, it has been quite lonely." And perhaps that was a failing of her own. Just another reason to seek out that man in the village and get up to scandal with him, to keep that feeling at bay. Letting emotions linger in her person wasn't something she particularly enjoyed, for it obscured entertainment and enjoyment of the present. "While I'm happy to stay in the country even though there are no compelling or delicious men here, I most certainly *will not* fall in love. I will hold out for as long as I can, so my life remains my own." At least being a governess would make certain she kept that vow. The vicar was quite old if she remembered correctly; she hadn't attended church in far too long.

Nora made a series of hand gestures. She shook her head and grinned. Out of all her sisters, she was perhaps the most stunning and beautiful. Ruby lips and cornflower blue eyes would enchant any man who happened upon her... if they could manage to understand her and provide the requisite patience and care she needed.

"Dear Nora." Gigi pulled a face. "If that means I am a spinster for the rest of my life, so be it, dear. That is not the worst thing a woman can be labeled."

"I agree with you." Her mother nodded. "Yet you are coming scandalously close to gaining a label from which you won't be able to recover your reputation."

Another huff of annoyance escaped her. "I am capable of guiding my own life." It was indeed her own, and she was quite content with that, as long as she could continue to kiss interesting men in shadowy corners or private spots throughout the country. "After all, how difficult could becoming a governess be? Regardless of my flirtatious behavior, I was quite astute in many subjects at school."

Her mother remained silent, but her eyes said that she expected Gigi to fail.

Emmaline smiled. "I think being a governess sounds lovely. Children are adorable."

"*Some* children," Gigi added as knots of concern pulled in her belly. *I'll show them all.* "Regardless, I should be home each evening to take dinner with you." At least it would be honest work for honest wages, and it would help her forget about life's responsibilities and worries. "That is, if the vicar is amenable to installing me in the position. He is quite aged, and from what I remember, he's apt to fall asleep at tea."

"Uh..." Anna frowned. "There is something you must know about the vicar—"

"Hush, Anna," her mother warned, with an odd expression on her face. "Genevieve has made it quite clear that she can manage her own life and her own choices. We should respect her wishes in that. She is perfectly capable of calling on the vicar and explaining why she is there."

A speaking glance was exchanged between them while Nora quickly signed something to their mother Gigi couldn't quite understand.

Bored with her embroidery, Gigi tossed it into the basket at her feet. "I suppose I should go upstairs and decide on a dress, for I intend to call on the vicar in the next couple of days." She looked at her sisters. "Do any of you wish to help me?"

Emmaline volunteered. "I will, and if we cannot find something in your wardrobe, perhaps Mia or Cora left something behind that will work."

"Thank you."

"And remember, Emmaline, Gigi can take care of herself. She needs no advice from us." With a slight smile Gigi didn't quite trust, her mother waved them both off. "If you have a chance, go out and gather a bouquet of wildflowers for our luncheon table. Perhaps that will cheer your father."

"I will, Mama." With a feeling of relief, Gigi quickly escaped the room with her youngest sister on her heels.

CHAPTER TWO

July 17, 1817
Hawthorn Cottage
Pavenham village
Bedfordshire, England

THE HONORABLE MR. Thomas Alderman—who had chosen to become a vicar, and in which case would be known as Mr. Alderman these days—sighed, for tea this afternoon was not going well.

Every day this week, he'd asked a couple of women—either from the village or beyond—in for tea as a way to interview them to possibly fill a governess position. So far, no one had stood out to him as able to take responsibility for his spirited nieces.

Today's candidates were an older woman, well known for being an easy-tempered grandmother to four in one village over from Pavenham, while the other was a meek and mild young lady who belonged to a titled family in a neighboring county. They were both polite and proper, both had lovely smiles, and both rarely met his gaze when he asked them a direct question.

Unfortunately, this meant his nieces would run right over them and rule the roost much as they did now.

To say nothing that the small whirlwinds worked to do their

darndest to make certain he didn't hire either of the women, but he'd made certain to have them both at tea because he simply had to keep an eye on them and he didn't want them outside in the garden digging up worms or worse.

With what he hoped was a stern glance at the two little raven-haired girls sitting on the sofa on the opposite side of the low table in the parlor, he rested his attention once more on the older woman. "Mrs. Barter, if you were to hold the governess position, how would you guide and mold my nieces so they will grow into proper members of society?"

This was especially important, for the girls were the granddaughters of Viscount Tetterfield, and that man had been his father. Thomas was the fourth child of said man; the girls were his sister's children.

After taking a sip from her cup, the older woman gently set it into the saucer and gave him a disarming smile. "I firmly believe that children should be seen but not heard. They shouldn't talk unless invited to do so. Otherwise, they are much too loud." When she set the cup and saucer on the table, she shifted her balance on the chair where she perched. "I would also add that at least three hours a day should be set aside to learn poise, decorum, and proper manners."

Across from him, his oldest niece, Penny, pulled a face and briefly stuck out her tongue.

Thomas bit the inside of his cheek to keep from grinning, for he didn't necessarily agree with the older woman's assessment. "How would you spend the remaining hours of a child's school day?"

"Of course, they would go through their paces in reading, writing, mathematics, as well as languages." Mrs. Barter chuckled and she clasped her hands together in her lap. "Of course, I don't expect Lily to keep such a rigorous schedule. She is much too young for some of these subjects, but she can be taught the value of silence and perhaps painting."

The girl in question, all of six years old, continued to dunk her fingers into her teacup and then sucked off the liquid while swinging her legs as she sat on her chair, apparently content.

Penny frowned. Clearly, she didn't enjoy that answer. "Why does Lily get to paint, and I don't? I like to paint. Water is my favorite thing to paint, and also dogs." Except Thomas had seen her attempts at dogs. They all had two legs for some reason, and he always wondered how the poor things kept their balance. "I don't want to be a proper lady."

"There is nothing more exceptional or sought after than a well-bred young woman who knows her place in the world," Mrs. Barter said to the girl, with a bit of a smug expression.

"I see. Thank you." Thomas drained the remainder of his cup and then set it into the saucer and laid them both on the table. Then he trained his attention on the other potential candidate. "What of you, Miss Lyle? What would you have the children study?"

The young woman's eyes lit when he said her name. Afternoon sunlight sparkled off her strawberry-blonde hair. "I believe that study should be equally intertwined with nurturing." She glanced at the girls, then back at him. "Though I do maintain the best role model for any young child under the age of ten is a mother as well as a father."

His chest unexpectedly tightened. "That is impossible for my nieces, Miss Lyle, but thank you for bringing up bad memories. Perhaps God wishes me to keep my roots and my outlook humble."

A hint of a blush stained her cheeks. "Oh, I do beg your pardon, Mr. Alderman. I meant no offense. I simply meant that perhaps you should marry. You and your wife could become surrogate parents for your nieces."

"Since I do not have plans to marry any time soon, this subject is moot." He frowned as he shot a glance at the two little girls. They certainly hadn't deserved the tragedy that had befallen the family, and though it had only been a year since their parents and his had perished in a horrific carriage accident on their way back to London, in many ways it felt as if it had happened just yesterday. "In the meanwhile, they have their uncles."

Except the girls had always been more comfortable in his presence over his older brothers, and his sister had been closest to him, which is why she'd wished for him to raise her children if something drastic ever occurred.

The young woman exchanged a glance with the older one, and she shrugged. "It would probably be in the girls' best interests if you do marry and settle down. They need the calming influence of a mother nonetheless."

A swift stab of annoyance went through his chest then he reminded himself to take a deep breath and ponder his words before he spoke. "Thank you for your concern, but we are doing well enough in the moment."

She batted her lashes. "And, if I may be so bold, a man as handsome as you shouldn't remain unattached. There are far too many women on the hunt in your congregation, I'll wager."

Give me strength and patience. Sadly, neither of these women were quite right in filling the open position.

When Penny giggled and clamped her linen napkin tightly into her lap, unease twisted down Thomas's spine.

"What have you got there, girl?" Mrs. Barter asked, for she was the closest to the girls' location. "Bring it here. Little girls shouldn't conceal things, and neither should they play tricks."

"I'm not doing either of those things," Penny protested, and her long black braids fairly quivered with outrage.

"Bring it here anyway." The older woman's voice didn't brook argument.

Without another word, Penny wriggled off the sofa, and with a glance at her sister, who looked properly horrified, she took the few steps to Mrs. Barter, where she then snapped open the napkin. Out tumbled a brown-green toad, which landed squarely in the older woman's lap.

"Awk!" The poor woman sprang to her feet while brushing the offensive amphibian from her person. Thomas scrambled to his feet at the same time. "Why in the world would an eight-year-old child have such a horrid thing in her possession?" She scrubbed at her clothing as if she could remove every trace of the toad. "Good heavens, it's staring at me!"

"Calm yourself, Mrs. Barter. Toads are basically harmless," Thomas said in a soothing voice, and then once more bit the inside of his cheek.

Meanwhile, the poor toad, no doubt upon being beyond bewildered, hopped away with an offended croak. Not that Thomas truly knew if an amphibian could become annoyed, but he liked to think that if he were a toad in the situation, he would indeed be offended. Once he went beneath a sofa, Thomas quietly expelled a breath of relief.

Penny, being Penny, merely grinned without malice or regret. "I found him down at the creek. If you want one, I can go find you one too."

"I should think not!" Mrs. Barter sent a glare around the occupants of the room. "I wouldn't take the position of governess, not even out of the goodness of my heart. The children are simply too far gone to be rehabilitated." Then, in high dudgeon, she flounced from the parlor. Seconds later, the front door to the vicarage slammed closed.

Miss Lyle eyed the floor where the toad was last seen. With haste, she stood and kept her skirting a bit above her ankles. "Well, I should go. No doubt you'll wish to give the girls a good talking to." She met his gaze with a smile that was slightly shaky. "If you find yourself in a bind with the children, I am available to help. Temporarily, I might add," she said and turned slightly green about the gills when the toad hopped onto the rug. "They should have someone to look after them until you can fill the governess position."

"Don't worry yourself about it, Miss Lyle. I'm sure that if the Creator wishes there to be a governess in our midst, someone will appear who has the proper constitution for it." Obviously, the last two candidates were not it. "I'll have one of the stable boys hitch your horse to your gig."

"Don't worry about it." She gestured to a young maid sitting in the corner that Thomas had forgotten about altogether. "Meg and I will go 'round to the barn and ask for assistance." When the toad turned about and croaked, she emitted a tiny squeak of alarm and bolted between the pieces of furniture. "Well, good day, Mr. Alderman. I wish you good fortune in your search."

"Thank you. Safe travels home." He walked behind the lady and her maid and saw them out of the cottage. As soon as he closed the door behind them, he returned to the parlor. "Girls, I think we should talk."

Penny huffed. "You mean you want to lecture us." She frowned at the toad. "I'm sorry I threw the toad on the woman. It was wrong, and it scared the toad."

Oh, God. I'm simply not somber enough to be a father figure.

"I agree that it was wrong. Not only from the toad's point of view, but also from Mrs. Barter's." He resumed his seat on the sofa and then gestured at the girls to join him. "Lily, did you have a part in bringing home the toad?"

"Not mostly, but I helped Penny put him in her pail." Once the little girl settled onto the cushion beside him, she curled into his side, and he lost his heart all over again for her. "Uncle Thomas, why must we have a governess?"

"I want to know too," Penny said, as she settled at his other side with the toad in her lap.

Yet another dress ruined because of her penchant for playing outside and mucking up her clothing, but he supposed the girls were allowed that small freedom after everything they'd already gone through.

"What happened today is *exactly* why you need a governess." Smoothing the escaped strands of black hair away from Penny's face, Thomas sighed. "As I tell you every time, you are the granddaughters of a viscount, and when you come of age, you will take your rightful places within the *beau monde*." The two little bodies, so trusting of him, and looking up at him with identical pairs of moss green eyes, nearly broke him. "That means you will eventually need to be proper young ladies, and in order to prepare for that, you need to practice proper behavior and deportment now. Unfortunately, it is beyond my ken to teach you that."

"But we don't want anyone else." Penny frowned. "Why can you not teach us? Mama said you were her favorite brother and that you always made her laugh."

Another tug to his heart brought out a wad of emotion into his throat. "While I appreciate that, there are some things in life only a lady can teach to girls." Had he already failed these precious little lives? Yes, it was slightly scandalous taking the girls in when he was a bachelor, and yes, they could have gone to his oldest and married brother who'd inherited the title when their father had died the same day the girls' parents had. But Robert didn't have the time or patience to give them—additionally, he had three children of his own—and neither would he have been present in their day-to-day existence. Robert resided in London for practical reasons, and that wasn't any place to raise girls of their nieces' temperaments. "However, I am becoming more and more busy with my growing congregation, and I don't want to neglect you."

It was Lily's turn to frown. "What is a congregation?"

"It is what I call my parishioners." Perhaps it was also another too-big-to-digest word, for he sighed and then grinned. "People who come to church."

"Oh." Then she put a tiny, delicate hand on his knee. "What is neglect?"

"It is when someone is doing something else instead of paying attention to those around him who mean... everything to him." In the girls, he constantly saw his sister, and every day that went by he was reminded of the enormity of his responsibility to them. "I love you and your sister far too much to not give you a proper education or care." Engaging a governess needed to happen soon, for the care of his congregation was beginning to suffer since his attention was distracted by his nieces.

A long-suffering sigh came from Penny, as if she carried the weight of the world on her little shoulders. "If we must have a governess, could she at least be fun?"

Despite himself, Thomas snorted. "I don't know if there is such a creature." His certainly hadn't been. But then, the poor women who'd held that position had been responsible for four rambunctious children—three of them boys—and if memory served correctly, none of them had lasted long. "However, I will try to find the perfect person to fill the post, but you must promise that you won't try and frighten her away with toads or worms or whatever tricks the two of you can concoct."

Both girls giggled, which intensified when the toad let out a croak and hopped beneath the sofa once more.

He continued, for it was important the girls understood the gravity of the situation. "Unless I can find a governess, you might need to go live with Uncle Robert in London." The man that Cynthia had married hadn't been of the *ton*. His only brother had died in the war, and apparently his parents had perished years earlier, for they had been older when they'd had their children.

Lily shook her head. "I do not like London. It's too noisy."

"And big," Penny added with a shiver. "There is nowhere to run and jump, and everyone frowns too much."

"Then it would behoove you to behave. I made your mother a promise that I would look after you to the best of my ability, but you must be willing to help." That had been a terrible day, when he'd rushed to the Derbyshire estate where his father's country seat was located, where his sister and her family had been visiting. As a result of the carriage accident on one of the rural roads, his parents had died instantly, but it had taken another few hours for Cynthia and her husband to succumb to their horrid injuries. Thomas hugged them both in turn. "Now, collect the toad and put him back where you found him. His family is probably looking for him. Afterward, we'll take a walk so you'll be hungry for dinner."

"Thank you, Uncle Thomas." Penny slipped from the sofa only to drop to all fours on the floor to reach beneath the sofa until she'd secured the toad.

"Try not to land into too much trouble." He slumped against the back of the sofa once the girls had both run from the room. "I think I'm in a spot of bother."

Not for the first time did he wonder if becoming a vicar and taking the living in this particular area had been a mistake. His life wasn't always walking the straight and narrow. For much of his past existence, he had been a rogue without a care in the world beyond his next entertainment or woman to take into his bed.

As the fourth child of a viscount and the third son, there had been no expectations placed upon him, and no one had given him direction for his life. Traditionally, such sons were instructed to either go into the military or the Church, and since he disliked anything having to do with the military or war, he'd considered the Church... and then summarily dismissed it in favor of squandering his life and chasing women.

Until the day he'd felt God call him to minister to those in need.

That shift and transition had been quite difficult, but in a way, cleaning up his life had given him the purpose he'd lacked before. It would be a lie to say that his good looks hadn't had a hand in growing his flock, but he was grateful for it. Additionally, the old vicar from whom he'd taken the living had cautioned him that he would need to marry sooner than later, for an unattached vicar could prove problematic and distracting.

Such a thing had been more or less true. There had been an uptick in flirting and interest in him as a person since he'd taken the living three years ago, to say nothing of the constant battle between his new life and his old one. In some ways, he missed the freedom he'd used to have, but being a vicar had given him a hopeful outlook he hadn't had before.

And then the girls had come to live with him, and everything changed once more. Perhaps becoming a vicar was his way of doing penance for all the scandal he'd conducted in his younger days, or perhaps it had happened to give him a fresh perspective on what the people in his congregation struggled with, but he didn't wish all of this to be yanked from his grasp merely due to the fact he couldn't find a woman to fill the governess position to his two lively nieces.

In this, as well as everything else, he would practice faith. If it were fated to come into being, it would. Until then, he had a sermon to write, and a walk with the girls to prepare for.

Please send us the woman who is most suited to look after the girls, and who will help us all come together better as a family.

CHAPTER THREE

July 20, 1817
Pavenham Church
Bedfordshire, England

G IGI SMOOTHED A hand down the front of her morning dress of plain ivory cambric. It featured surplice sleeves, and a Vandyke border around the throat. Not exactly the style of dress she enjoyed wearing, for it felt as if she would be strangled at any moment, and there was no hope of showing any sort of décolletage, but then, she supposed attending church wasn't exactly the time and place for flirting. A Spanish robe of sky-blue crepe bordered with darker blue cambric trimming completed the look. She fussed with the buttons on the robe then touched a hand to the detestable beehive bonnet of plaited straw, ornamented with ribbons in various shades of blue, done by her own hand. Matching sky-blue kid slippers completed the ensemble.

Though she hadn't attended church services for more years than she cared to remember, the one thing she *did* recall was that bonnets were never removed, and that meant she'd have no choice but to sit there with the hideous thing on her head.

Out of all the rules that kept women downtrodden that she despised the most, wearing a bonnet ranked up there with the big ones. It kept her from seeing everything she needed to see, and it certainly wasn't one bit attractive.

However, it was necessary if she wanted to speak with the vicar after the services, for the more she'd thought upon the manner, the more pleasing the position of governess seemed. She would have her evenings and nights free, and it would be lovely to have a bit of coin to spend on herself for a change. Finally, she could purchase new gowns in the hopes of attracting a man of substance.

With no more time to linger, Gigi entered the small church. Long, polished wood pews filled a good portion of the main room. A wooden divider went down the middle of the room, separating the pews. The ends at the sides of the room were open. By and large, the bulk of the congregation was female, of all ages, and every one of them had expressions of anticipation.

That was exceedingly odd. The last time she attended church services, she didn't find them all that exciting. As she slipped into the front pew on the right, she smiled at two small girls who were sitting quietly side by side, one with a stuffed rag dog and one who held a doll that had a porcelain head and hands. Both wore their black hair in braids that looked rather the worse for wear, but their white ruffled dresses were cleaned and pressed, and the girls were adorable. But where were their parents? As of yet, no adult had come to sit beside them.

When would the vicar make an appearance? She didn't know much about him. Growing up, the vicar in the village was an older man who often forget his train of thought and sometimes fell asleep in his study when he should have been attending tea at someone's house. As she'd dressed this morning, her sister Anna had sneaked into her bedchamber and told her the old man was no longer in charge of the church, that three years ago, a younger man had taken the position and he was pleasant enough.

A murmur of excitement wove through the congregation. Seconds later, a man emerged from a door behind the pulpit. As he ascended the few steps then took a position behind the podium, Gigi couldn't help but stare.

"Good morning. It is lovely to see all of you today." His voice was a rich baritone that sent a surprising little shiver down her spine.

This was Vicar Alderman? He was nothing like the older vicar. In fact, he was… delicious. While he gave a good morning message, Gigi looked her fill of him.

Thick black hair that trended to curls had been slightly tamed by pomade, which he did not need. She could easily imagine that hair with the wind rippling through it. Clear, gray eyes were intriguing. Would they darken like a summer storm under high emotion? When Vicar Alderman began his sermon, she gloried in the sound of his voice. Would that she could close her eyes and imagine the sweet nothings such a man might whisper into a lady's ear under cover of midnight. Her pulse increased, for his jaw was rather on the rugged side, and those lips! How could two pieces of flesh appear so sensual even when talking about the words of God? Far too amused, Gigi continued to study him. Standing at perhaps nearly six feet, he was lean and fit, and the possibilities of how he kept himself in such a condition swept her away with far too many scenarios in her imagination.

How interesting! It seemed the village had been hiding this man all too well from her, and in the same vein, how had she never seen such a stunning man before?

While he continued with his sermon, the words escaped her, for she was content enough merely to watch his mouth and how his lips formed words. What would a kiss from this man feel like? Then she was obliged to tamp down on the urge to giggle; such thoughts were wildly inappropriate, especially about a man of God.

A few minutes later, the two little girls not far from her on the pew entered into an argument over the stuffed dog the smaller of them had in her lap. Their voices continued to rise, and from the murmurs of dissent around her, they proved a tad disruptive. Racked with indecision, Gigi glanced upward into the pulpit at the vicar. Disappointment lined his face as she gave the girls a speaking glance, and she was near enough to see the panic in his eyes.

Ah. They must be his nieces.

When the squabbling didn't stop, Gigi made a decision. Once she'd moved along the pew, she took the younger girl's hand. "Come with me, you two. This is far too much noise during the sermon."

Identical expressions of surprise appeared on the girls' faces, but they gathered their toys and then followed her out of the pew and along the side aisle. As more than a few people stared at them, Gigi ignored them and herded the children outside the church. She had no right, of course, but perhaps that would be her opportunity to talk with the vicar.

Since she had no idea where the vicarage was located, she escorted the girls down the lane and then across the main road into a meadow filled with tall, sweet grasses and wildflowers. "This looks like a pretty place to sit and have a chat." Once she reached a cluster of oak trees, she gestured to the girls. "Settle yourselves. We shall talk until the service is finished."

Oddly enough, they both sat beneath the trees with her, and crossed their legs Turkish-style, with apparently no regard for their stocking-clad legs that were on display, and waited with expectation while Gigi did the same. And no, she didn't give two braces that her own legs were on display or that there was far too much ankle exposed. In fact, she removed her slippers and set them beside her.

"How often do you disrupt the sermon on Sundays?" Truly, that was what she wanted to know first, for in that one little glimpse of their lives, they reminded Gigi of herself at those ages.

The girls glanced at each other, and when the youngest tried to take the doll from the oldest, they erupted into a squabble once more.

"Stop!" Instinct rose in her being, and knowing the only way to head off further conflict was to confiscate the distractions, she easily plucked both the rag dog and the doll from lax fingers and stuffed them both into her lap. "Now, let us begin again, shall we?"

Both girls blinked at her with rounded eyes.

Gigi heaved a sigh. They didn't trust adults. No matter. She didn't consider herself an adult most days, and certainly didn't feel like one. "All right, we shall start at the beginning. My name is Genevieve, but my sisters and friends refer to me as Gigi."

The youngest girl tittered. "That's a funny name."

"Perhaps. What is your name? I might wish to laugh at it." One of her eyebrows rose in challenge.

"Um…" The little girl shot her sister a look, and the older one shrugged. "My name is Lily. Miss Lily Kingsley."

"Lily is a lovely name." Gigi smiled. She untied the ribbons beneath her chin as she glanced at the other girl. "And who are you?"

"Miss Penny Kingsley," the girl said promptly, with a nod.

"Good. At least you have some manners, and aren't the wild hoydens I first assumed." When she removed her bonnet, she laid the headgear on top of her slippers. "I am Miss Hasting, and believe it or not, I *was* a hoyden at your age. Even beyond that." Then she winked. "Not that I think there is anything wrong with a young lady being a hoyden, but I suspect whoever is in charge of you has grave misgivings."

Penny snorted at that, which was interesting. Perhaps she understood sarcasm and conversation well above her age group. "Does *hoyden* mean running all over the countryside and picking up toads?"

"It can in some circumstances." She rested her gaze on the younger of the girls. "It can also mean trying to take toys that don't belong to you, or climbing on furniture, then jumping off after you've been told not to."

Lily's lower jaw dropped open. "How do you know I do that?"

"Ah, because I'm magical." Gigi tapped her temple as she

grinned. "And I have done everything scandalous you can already think of. Therefore, I know all the trouble you will try to fall into." She shrugged. "It's a skill not many women have." When the girls remained silent, she continued. "To whom do you belong?"

"We are Thomas's nieces," Lily said promptly.

"I see." Though she did not. "Who is Thomas?"

Lily giggled. "The vicar. He is our uncle, and he doesn't like that we are wild."

"He doesn't." It wasn't a question. "What does he wish you were?"

Penny blew out a breath of frustration. "Proper young ladies." Then she pointed her gaze to the leaves above their heads and flicked her raven braid over her shoulder. "He says that granddaughters of a viscount shouldn't comport themselves like we do."

That would make the delicious looking vicar the son of a viscount. How interesting. "Well, he's not wrong." When the girls began a protest, she held up a gloved hand. "But he's not entirely right either." It wasn't her place to tell these two anything, for her perspective could make their behavior worse, but they clearly needed some sort of advice. "The trick is to be proper *sometimes* and then, when no one is looking, be as wild as you want. As long as it doesn't reach your uncle's ears, there is no harm."

I am probably going to hell.

Penny frowned. "Were you wild as a little girl?"

"More than you can even imagine." It was Gigi's turn to giggle. "My poor parents nearly washed their hands of me. My governesses constantly lectured me, but none of that could correct my behavior." She hadn't cared for rules then, and she certainly didn't now that she knew about the world and how unfair it was for women. "After that, I was sent away to finishing school, where there is nothing but rules, lectures, and learning how to dance and be all the proper things a lady should be."

"What did you do?" Lily asked.

"What could I do? My father is a baron. We don't live too far from here. I had to attend finishing school. After that, my parents took us to London where they rented a townhouse so I could have a few Seasons along with my sisters."

"What is a Season?" Penny wanted to know.

"It is a time when a young lady attends balls and parties for the express purpose of finding a husband." Gigi sighed. "The richer the better, really. Society thinks there isn't much use for a woman except to marry, have babies, and keep house. If that is so, then I say there should be vast amounts of coin at hand to buy fripperies and things that will make said life a bit more fun."

Oh, dear. I shouldn't have said that.

"Are you married?"

Gigi rested her gaze solidly on the older girl. "I am not."

"Why not?" Lily wanted to know.

Why indeed? "My sisters say I'm too picky and my mother says I'm chasing scandal too much when I should concentrate on attracting a man." She shrugged and plucked a random flower from the grass, then she tucked the bloom into the doll's hair. "The trouble, I suspect, is that I'm having too much fun flirting with the wrong sorts of men because I'm not certain I believe in love."

Was that true? And if it were, why was she confessing such a thing to the little girls?

With all the seriousness of a much older woman, Penny nodded. "I just want to wear pretty gowns and drink champagne to see if the bubbles tickle my nose."

"Fair enough, and in the event you wondered, both are quite lovely." Gigi shook her head. She was a poor role model and should probably stop talking to these girls. "Your uncle was trying to do his sermon when you two interrupted him with your squabbling. That wasn't well done of you."

"But we were bored," Penny countered, but sputtered to a stop when Gigi held up a hand.

"That matters not. It takes great courage to stand up in front of people and talk about what a person believes in, especially your uncle." She sighed, for she saw herself many times over in these girls. "If nothing else, he deserves your respect." Though she didn't know the full story of how the girls came to be with him, it was no doubt a sorrowful one.

Lily blew out a breath. "There is nothing to do when Uncle Thomas says his sermons."

"I understand that. Next time, perhaps bring a picture book with you." Silence brewed between them. "When I was your age, one of my sisters taught me how to make chains with daisies. Would you like to do that right now while we wait for your uncle?"

Both girls nodded.

"Good. Go gather a bunch of daisies—the white flowers with yellow middles—as well as Black Eyed Susans—yellow flowers with brown middles—and bring them back here."

It took next to no time for the girls to accomplish the task. Soon enough, they brought back armfuls of the flowers, then Gigi showed them how to knot the stems and link the blooms together. After a few false starts and several broken stems or flower heads that popped off, the girls mastered the skill.

"Excellent! Now just make it as long as you'd like," Gigi said with an encouraging nod. "You can even wrap the chain double for your crowns. The more times around you go, the fuller it will be."

"This is fun," Lily remarked as her nimble fingers worked the flower stems as fast as her sister's.

"I always found it so," Gigi said in response. At least it kept the girls entertained.

Eventually, the flower chains were completed. She taught them how to twist the strands about their heads and secure them into crowns. Against their black hair, the flowers served as a wonderful contrast. When she did the same to hers, both girls giggled and said she looked like a fairy princess.

"The good thing about making daisy crowns is that whenever the first one has died, you can always make another, fresh one. Throughout the summer, there will never be a shortage of flowers, and flower crowns are much better to wear than stuffy old bonnets." *That is probably another thing I shouldn't have told them.* Then Gigi put the finishing touches on their morning by showing them how to knot a daisy stem and fashion it into a ring. She held out her hand with one of the Black Eyed Susans acting as a gemstone on her finger. "You'll always be rich when you have flowers."

Penny was suitably impressed. "How do you know what to do with flowers?"

"Well, I have five sisters. We had to find things to do whenever we were in the country, and there are plenty of meadows filled with flowers." Gigi shrugged and smiled. "If you know where to go, you'll find yourself bored outside, and sometimes it's fun to bring painting supplies out here. I've no talent for it myself like my sister Nora, but I can create a passable landscape."

The younger sister stared at her with round eyes and much awe. "Do you like toads, Miss Hasting?"

"Well, I don't hate them, but I wouldn't go out of my way to search them out." She chuckled, for it had been a pleasant hour with these two. "I am more apt to play with barn cats or run with hunting dogs. Sometimes, I enjoy catching butterflies or even watching rabbits."

Movement in the meadow captured Gigi's attention, and flutters moved through her lower belly when she caught sight of the vicar. He was quite handsome in a black suit of simple design as well as a top hat.

"It seems as though our time together has come to an end, for your uncle has found us."

"Oh." Though Penny frowned, she scrambled to her feet as the vicar joined them beneath the trees. "Hullo, Uncle Thomas."

Thomas. Gigi tumbled his name over in her mind. It suited him. Plain, simple, and strong.

"Hullo, Penny." He shifted his gaze to the younger girl. "Lily." A faint frown took possession of his sensual lips, and once more Gigi's attention dropped to his mouth. "I was extremely disappointed in the both of you for interrupting the sermon."

"Penny wouldn't share her doll," Lily began, but when Gigi softly cleared her throat, she immediately sprang to her feet. "I'm sorry."

The vicar's eyes rounded. "Thank you. I appreciate that." Then he swung his gaze to her, and heat went through her cheeks. "Can I say this is your doing?"

When he offered a gloved hand to her, Gigi slipped her fingers into his palm and let him assist her into a standing position. "Partially. They were a bit unruly, but then, young children are unsuited to an adult sermon, and an hour to sit without squirming is rather an eternity for them."

"Ah." He held her hand a few seconds longer than necessary. "Well, I thank you. There are a handful of people in my congregation who don't appreciate my nieces attending the sermons, but I have nowhere else to put them."

The girls tittered and exchanged glances. Then Penny stepped forward and tugged at the vicar's hand. "We were excited about meeting Miss Hasting. Can she please be our governess? She has so many ideas and is ever so fun."

"Oh?" His dark eyebrows rose in surprise. "I thought you both didn't want a governess."

Lily grinned. "We want her. She isn't stodgy or stiff or ancient, and she doesn't smell like joint poultice." The girl touched her fingertips to the daisy crown on her head. "She taught us how to make these." Dropping her voice to the world's worst stage whisper, she said, "Miss Hasting said she was magical."

That struck Gigi as funny, but she tamped down the urge to laugh. "Well, at least that is a decent endorsement."

"Perhaps all of that is true, for no one has been able to tame you girls." Once more, he glanced at her, and those clear gray eyes seemed to peer into her soul. What would he find if that were true? "Come to the vicarage with us, Miss Hasting. We can share tea and perhaps have a much-needed talk."

Since she had hoped for an audience with him regardless, she nodded. "Very well, Mr. Alderman, and thank you." After she grabbed her bonnet and slipped on her shoes, she followed him out from beneath the trees. Lily slipped her hand into Gigi's. There was something so comforting and... happy in holding a child's hand, and for whatever reason, tears temporarily welled in her eyes.

For good or for ill, this might be a new path for her to trod. Would it bring the contentment or stop the feelings of restlessness plaguing her? Only time would tell.

CHAPTER FOUR

B Y THE TIME Thomas had led the small party through the meadow, the only thing occupying his mind was the subtle scent of lilies of the valley that wafted from Miss Hasting's direction, as well as how fetching she looked with the crown of daisies upon her blonde head.

"I haven't seen you at Sunday services recently," he said as a way to introduce a conversation while Penny chattered about everything and anything at his side.

The dulcet sound of her soft laughter sent awareness skittering over his skin. "That is due to the fact that I haven't attended church in years."

"Ah." How interesting. "Did you have a bad experience in the past, or do you not believe in God's love?"

"That is a difficult question that doesn't require an either-or answer." Every once in a while, she would lift the hem of her skirting to avoid taller weeds or the occasional stick that poked up from the ground. The tantalizing glimpse of her stocking-clad ankles captivated his mind. "Suffice it to say I have never found church services all that stimulating and would much rather spend that time doing something I enjoy."

"I am sorry to hear that, for I strive to write sermons that aren't dull or pompous." When he turned his head and met her gaze, he wanted nothing more than to fall into the deep blue pools of her eyes before he firmly shoved such thoughts away. He wasn't that man any longer.

"You don't seem to have issues filling your church. No doubt it's your looks that help with that and not the content of your sermons." Stated in such a matter-of-fact way, the words took a bit of his confidence. "I'll wager you don't hurt for female companionship."

This was hardly the conversation to have while his nieces were listening. "The congregation has steadily grown in the past few years that I've had the living. I try my best to keep the flock engaged."

Penny tugged on his hand. "Why is it your flock?"

Never one to pass on a learning moment, Thomas grinned. "In the Bible, Jesus referred to his followers as his flock, which is a direct reference to the relationship between a shepherd and his sheep."

The little girl frowned. "You have sheep?"

"In a manner of speaking. It's a parable. Jesus took care of his followers as a shepherd looks after his sheep. If one gets lost, he will search for it and nurture it back to health. Such is the same with me as a vicar and my congregation. I care for my parishioners."

"Oh." She swung his hand. "Is Miss Hasting a part of your flock?"

"I would like her to be, but I will discuss that with her later." Yes, he'd dedicated his life to serving God and his parishioners, he wasn't so taken by zeal like the evangelicals who were gaining a foothold within religion throughout England. He liked to think of his style as somewhere in the moderate middle, employing slight emotion in his sermons and hoping the congregation would join him in his charitable endeavors that looked after widows, orphans, as well as men who returned from war and needed assistance. "However, if you would like to entice Miss Hasting into our flock, you should practice proper behavior."

Penny huffed out a breath. "I will try but I can't promise to behave. It is quite dull."

From his other side, Miss Hasting attempted to quell a snort of laughter, but she was only half successful. "Unfortunately for you, Mr. Alderman, I tend to agree with her."

"Then it is my sworn duty to change your mind, Miss Hasting."

Once more, he glanced at her and was struck by how dainty and feminine the sky-blue dress was, and how it brought out the blue in her eyes and made her skin fairly glow with good health. Though the cut of the dress was modest in deference of attending church, somehow on Miss Hasting, she made it all too seductive, which in many ways was more effective than curve-hugging fabric or a low neckline.

She was sin and scandal—exactly the type of woman he would have pursued in his past life as a rogue.

"Miss Hasting?" This from Lily.

"Yes?"

"Is it proper to wear a daisy crown to tea?"

Miss Hasting briefly glanced at him before settling her attention on the little girl. "I think for today, it is entirely proper and even encouraged, for flowers were made from God and will provide something pretty to brighten up an otherwise ordinary tea."

"Thank you." It was Lily's wide smile and sparkling eyes that tugged at Thomas's heart.

He hadn't seen either of his nieces so animated in a long time indeed. How incredibly fortuitous that Miss Hasting had come into their lives when she did. Would she be amenable to taking a governess position? At the moment, he knew little about her or her family, even if he'd taken tea with her parents a couple of times in the past.

Eventually, the vicarage came into view, and he grinned, for the cottage rested about half a mile away on the other side of the meadow and lay tucked into a stand of woods with a babbling brook that ran through the property.

"Welcome to Hawthorn Cottage, Miss Hasting," he said as he pushed open the door and ushered them up a garden path. The fragrance of many different flowers wafted to his nostrils. The buzz from bees and other insect life that thrived on the blooms provided a pleasant backdrop as they strolled to the house. "It's a quaint and cozy home, quite a different residence than what I was used to in the past."

With a roof made to look like thatch but made of stronger materials and lower ceilings complete with dark beams and a large hearth in the main living room, it had a certain charm about it that made him think of simpler times and easier days than the modern world currently offered.

In the tiny entryway, he paused to hang his top hat on a hook and then took Miss Hasting's bonnet from her fingers and hung it up as well. To the girls, he said, "Go upstairs and ask one of the maids to help you change clothes. I don't know how they will remove the grass stains on those dresses, but I believe in everyday miracles. I shall call you down when it's time for luncheon."

As the girls ran along the narrow corridor to a set of wooden stairs at the back of the cottage, he led Miss Hasting into the room to the left of the hallway, which was a formal parlor where he met with parishioners for tea and talking.

"Please settle yourself, Miss Hasting. If you wish, we can begin the interview straightaway."

"What?" A frown pulled the corners of her lips downward, which only served as a distraction for him. In his former life, he would have used this brief time alone as a thin excuse to steal a kiss. "An interview for what?" But the slight sparkle in her eyes betrayed the fact she already knew.

"For the governess position." He gestured her toward a low sofa. "By the by, since we weren't formally introduced, I'm Mr. Alderman."

"Right. And of course, I'm Miss Hasting." When she perched on the edge of the piece of furniture, Thomas sat in a matching chair near her location. "Perhaps we should start with what you truly thought when you saw me remove your nieces from the church."

Well, she wasn't shy, he'd give her that. With an indulgent chuckle, he leaned back in his chair. "I was alternately pleased and appalled. The girls do have a tendency to interrupt my sermons more often than not, but no other person in the congregation took the initiative like you did." What had prompted that decision? "Why did you take them into the meadow? You could have escorted them home or sat on the bench in the garden of the church."

A faint blush stained her cheeks. "Since I haven't attended services for a few years, I had no idea about the garden, nor did I know where the vicarage was located." She clasped her fingers in her lap. "The meadow seemed a logical place where the girls could run if they wished or entertain themselves with the flowers, and the shade from the trees was quite refreshing."

"I can understand that; the three of you seemed much relaxed when I came upon you." Again, he couldn't help but study her, and in this setting, she was even more alluring. Her blonde upswept hair glimmered with various shades of gold. "Yet even in that, you have shown yourself well-versed and quite comfortable with scandal. You wore no bonnet, took no maid as a chaperone." He shrugged. And she was past the first and second blushes of youth. "What have you to say of that?"

"There is nothing to say. I dislike bonnets and maids trailing after me." When she shrugged, the dress pulled taut briefly across her modest breasts. "Just as I despise society's rules, men with no spine, and everything a lady must do to be considered 'proper' in the very narrow view of that word."

"Ah." She was well spoken, and he appreciated that. "Have you ever considered taking a paid position as a governess?" Perhaps she didn't wish to dirty her hands with work. "I've met with your parents only a couple of time since taking this living, but from what I could glean, they are nearly in dun territory."

Had that crossed a line?

"That is true. The taxes on Landover Manor haven't been paid in years. Eventually, it will be taken from my parents, but my father's faculties are slowly leaving him. There is nothing he can do about either situation." She clasped her fingers more tightly, and as he continued to study her, he caught sight of a small, port-wine birthmark on the inside of her left arm, just above the elbow, that looked like an abstract strawberry. "Our family's circumstances are no secret; it was why we have no longer go to London in recent years, why my sisters and I all live with my parents."

"I'm sorry to hear of your father's health worries. I shall make a point to call on him and your mother soon." Life was always changing and evolving, and he took the concerns of his congregation seriously.

"Thank you." Miss Hasting nodded. "As for my qualifications for a governess position, I was the third daughter and my parents adopted two younger girls. Sometimes, it was required of me to look after them." A tiny giggle snuck into her explanation, and the sound was quite melodious. "To say nothing of the fact that I spent copious time sneaking away from *my* governesses. This gives me a unique understanding of a child's mind."

"I am familiar with your younger sisters, or at least one of them. Anna, I believe, does odd jobs in the village for some of my parishioners who are unable to get out and about."

"Yes, Anna likes to keep herself busy, and in doing so, she hopes no one will notice her scarred face." Sorrow filled Miss Hasting's eyes. "I fear for their future, for what they went through during the fire that took their parents' lives was horrific."

"Sudden tragedy usually is." He couldn't help but think about what happened in his own life that landed his nieces into his care. "Are you older sisters married?" But what he really wanted to know was why she wasn't.

"Yes." She nodded and then raised her gaze to his. "I suppose you weren't here when Mia married in the spring, and Cora must have asked the old vicar to marry her over a month or so ago." A sigh escaped her. "Before that, they'd taken positions as paid companions in London, which precipitated their meeting their respective husbands."

It was all far too interesting, and he asked the question anyway. "Yet here you are, not married. Why is that? Surely someone would have asked for your hand by now." He chuckled, for how could they not? "You are still young, have your looks, come from a good family, though impoverished. One would think with the recent marriages, more scrutiny would have been put on the remaining and single Hasting sisters."

"Well, that is a disappointment." Annoyance threaded through her voice.

"What? The fact you are not married?"

"No! I'm disappointed that you assume it's the only thing a woman aspires to… marriage, being a mother, keeping a house." She shook her head as fury flashed in her eyes. "Men might have a limited view of the world we live in, but that doesn't mean women don't have other purposes if only they were given a shred of an opportunity." Her voice rose with each sentence. "And those opportunities are severely limited here in the country."

"Easy, Miss Hasting." Thomas put up a hand in surrender. "My apologies. I didn't mean to offend." Although, he now wondered what had happened in her life to make her so defensive.

"Thank you." After taking a deep breath and then releasing it, she continued. "I'm quite content in being a spinster and I enjoy getting into scandal where I can." Her gaze never dropped as she looked at him, and he admired the forthrightness as well. "Societal rules are too stifling and I don't wish to marry, for that would mean my life would no longer be my own. Everything that I have would suddenly belong to him; my individual identity would vanish, and I would become an extension of him." Truth rang in those words, and he'd wager the small amount of coin he had that she'd never admitted such to anyone. "Marrying would give a man too much power over me, and I am not keen on that… unless he wants to do so in the bedroom."

"Ah." The words as well as the images that danced through his mind of her entwined in the sheets of his bed sent heat sailing up the back of his neck as well as racing along his shaft. Though he was wildly embarrassed, he was also on his way to being fully aroused.

On a Sunday morning.

While his nieces played upstairs.

"I will admit, that wasn't the most proper of things to say to a vicar and one who is seeking a governess for his nieces. I apologize. Women's rights and expectations, or lack thereof, is a sore subject for me."

"So I have surmised."

"Good. Just so we are clear on that." When Miss Hasting grinned, his world tilted.

God save me, for she is far too tempting. Yet he ignored every warning alarm that rang in his head to return to the matter at hand. "What subjects are you able to teach with authority for the girls?" *Or more to the point, what can you teach me?* It would only take one kiss to know…

For one second, she bit her bottom lip before releasing it. Interest flickered in her eyes. "Geography, grammar, reading—I love to read and unfortunately Papa sold off most of our books—I can speak French, a bit of Italian, I remember some Latin from my own school days, but other than that, I'm afraid I'm a dunce. Especially at numbers. Mia was given that gift."

The woman was a spitfire, and suddenly there was a thread of excitement back in his life that he'd been missing ever since taking the living… since his sister and parents died. Thomas nodded. "What of deportment?"

She frowned. "Surely the girls are too young for those lessons."

"I used to think along the same lines, but each month that goes by shows me that they desperately need those lessons." He paused, leaned forward, and rested his elbows on his knees, steepling his fingers. "They are a viscount's grandchildren, and wards of a vicar. Deportment and at the very least manners are something desperately needed. I'm afraid if you cannot do that, then I cannot in good conscience hire you on—"

"Fine!" Miss Hasting waved a hand. "I shall teach the girls deportment, even though I don't believe in women being so repressed when men can do whatever they like without recrimination."

Oh, dear God, she would prove a handful even without the children. And if he weren't careful, he'd fall back into his wicked ways, the very ones he tried so hard to put behind him.

I must be a fool to even consider letting this woman become a governess.

Slowly, she rose to her feet. "If you intend to hire me, I can walk over to be with the girls by nine each morning—"

"Actually, this is a live-in position, Miss Hasting," he was quick to interrupt as he surged into a standing position. "I am often out visiting my parishioners and involving myself with charities and such. When I am not doing that, then I am studying and working at writing my Sunday sermon. Someone needs to watch the girls and look after them all the time, and my housekeeper has threatened to give notice if she must have the raising of them any longer."

"I see." For a few seconds, it appeared as if she would flee the room, and the way she glanced out the window made him think she valued her freedom, but then she nodded. "What of the living arrangements?"

Thomas cleared his throat, for it only just occurred to him that they would sleep beneath the same roof, and she was clearly not an older woman or a widow, perhaps with a wart on her chin. "The cottage is big enough that we won't be in each other's way." His swallow was audible. "There are two small bedrooms as well as a slightly larger one upstairs that I occupy. You are welcome to the empty one." Fairly tripping over his words, he rushed onward. "If it's too improper, I will sleep in my office down here right off the living area. You can use the attic for a schoolroom."

"The attic?" Another frown turned her pink lips downward. "That space will be terribly hot. It's the summer, and the countryside is beautiful this time of year. When it's not raining, I shall conduct my lessons outside." When she looked at him with those unfathomable blue eyes that glimmered with wicked promise, he should have taken back his offer. "I doubt you will find objection to this, since we should all be admiring and enjoying God's creation, yes?"

"Absolutely we should." Yes, she would be trouble. Far too much tempting, scandalous trouble. Was he strong enough to withstand her charm? Thomas straightened his spine. He was, of course he was. Hadn't he renounced that roguish lifestyle, and hadn't he taken up the reins of being a man of God?

He didn't miss that life at all.

Much.

CHAPTER FIVE

July 24, 1817
Hawthorn Cottage

IT HAD BEEN four days since the vicar had hired her on as governess to his nieces, and three days since she'd been installed in his cottage. Though her home and family were a mere mile's walk away, in some hours it felt as if she were on an island somewhere surrounded by an unfamiliar sea; Gigi had been wildly unprepared for the task before her.

The girls, while sweet and silly most of the time, had hard tendencies to be stubborn and willful at others. Already there had been disagreements between her and them, a few rounds of tempestuous tears on both her part and that of the girls, but there had been lovely moments as well. There would be growing pains from all parties until some sort of schedule could be undertaken.

Above all, Gigi was determined to succeed in the position because her mother had given her a parting lecture and an admonition to behave herself, for the village didn't need her leading either the vicar or his nieces into scandal. If that happened, it might be the final rumor that broke her father's spirit.

Since it was a Wednesday, apparently the vicar was out visiting various widows throughout the village and its surrounds. He dropped off baskets of foodstuffs and checked on the older folks to make certain they were doing well. That meant Gigi was alone with the girls, so she asked the housekeeper to pack them a picnic lunch and then she took the children outside in search of a small pond she remembered from her own childhood.

"Where are we going?" Penny was content to walk alongside Gigi, for any day they weren't in a classroom was an adventure to her.

"To a pond."

"Why?"

"Do you remember the paper boats we made before leaving the house?" It was a skill she'd gleaned years ago from her father, when he'd taken her and her sisters out to the same pond to sail the same boats.

"Yes." Befuddlement lay stamped over the girl's face.

"Well, we are going to sail the boats. It's fine weather for it, don't you think?"

"I suppose…" Penny frowned. "But what will that teach us?"

Gigi shrugged. "That you should enjoy the sunshine while you have it. That being outside makes a person much more likely to feel thankful for God than sitting in an uncomfortable church pew, that we will identify at least five species of flowers on our walk to and from the pond, that if we're fortunate, we might find both a toad and a frog so you can see the difference between the two." Gigi turned her head and winked at the girl. "And that if there is no wind, our boats won't be able to traverse the surface of the pond, proving it doesn't take as much skill to sail as pirates wish us to believe."

Penny's lips formed an *o* of awe. Then she nodded. "You are quite wise, Miss Hasting."

"I don't know about that." But she did have experience in not being a proper lady, so perhaps it was the same thing. She glanced at Lily. "What say you, Lily? Does sailing paper boats sound like fun?"

"I would rather make flower wreaths again." As she spoke,

the girl plucked a bloom from the grass. "May we do that?"

"Of course. The afternoon is for the full enjoyment of the outside world."

And perhaps it would prevent Gigi from thinking about the vicar who was more handsome than he had a right to be. Never in her life had she held an interest in a man of the cloth, but there was something about him that stirred awareness of him as a man. Did she desire him? Oh, yes. Did she want to find out if she could perhaps seduce him into scandal? Very much so, but as of yet, she hadn't decided how to do that without jeopardizing her position. Unintentionally, she'd grown fond of the girls, and felt for their circumstances.

They arrived at the pond in short order, and as soon as the paper boats were placed upon the water, they sailed for a few feet before the water saturated them and they started to sink, but what held Gigi's attention were the pair of brown geese and an errant white swan who currently sauntered toward her.

"Perhaps we should keep moving," she told the girls in a low voice. It was that she didn't like waterfowl, but she didn't trust them.

Lily moved behind her. "Will they hurt us?"

"I don't believe so." It was past time for either of the species to sit on eggs, and it didn't appear there were young goslings or cygnets about, but that didn't mean they weren't hiding. No matter how many steps away from the birds she took, the three of them continued to follow while making low sounds of interest instead of umbrage. "Move away slowly if you'd like, and I'll see if I can distract them."

As the girls moved a few feet ahead, the geese and the swan merely eyed them with boredom, but the second Gigi took a few steps forward, the birds followed. The geese made soft honking noises, and when she tried running ahead of the girls, the waterfowl came right along with her at a fast clip.

"Well, I guess we know who they're interested in," she said with a wry grin, much to the children's amusement. Many giggles ensued. Heat filled her cheeks. "What do I do now?"

Penny snorted. "Make the best of it, Miss Hasting."

"Perhaps I should, but in the meanwhile, let us lay down our blankets in a shady spot and I'll let you make daisy chains again. Then we'll have our picnic."

The tasks were accomplished, and a large oak tree provided more than enough shade. She let the girls remove their shoes and stockings so they could put their feet into the very edges of the pond while hunting for amphibians while Gigi watched them from the relative safety of the blankets. Apparently agreeing with the need for some relaxation, the pair of geese took up a position off to one side and settled in for a nap. The swan returned to the water, but kept paddling nearby, and occasionally, it would look over to make certain Gigi was still there.

How truly odd.

As the middle of the day progressed, the sun made them all drowsy. Eventually, the girls returned to the campsite. Bread, cheese, and fruit was passed around, as was cold chicken and ham, and bottles of lemonade. Afterward, everyone partook of jam tarts and a few tiny seed cakes the housekeeper had tucked into the basket, for they were Lily's favorite.

"Mama used to enjoy these cakes," the little girl said into the silence, as she lounged on her belly and nibbled at the last cake.

"Did she?" Gigi held her breath. Would she wish to speak of her parents?

"Yes." Lily nodded. She frowned as she focused on Gigi's face. "I miss her."

"There is nothing wrong with that." She folded her legs at the knee, tucked them beneath her skirting, and offered what she hoped was an encouraging smile. "From what I have heard from your uncle, it's been a year since you lost your parents." It wasn't a question.

Penny nodded and spoke before her sister could. "I didn't like that time."

"I can imagine you did not." When she reached for the girl's hand, Penny shied away. Which was expected, for they didn't know each other all that well. "What did you like most about your parents?"

"They always laughed and smiled."

"That's a lovely memory." Life was always better when the people around a person were laughing instead of grouchy. "It's the silence that is confusing when you're used to talking and laughing."

"Our grandparents died with Mama and Papa," Penny confided in a soft voice with a frown. She focused her gaze on the lemonade bottle in her hand.

"Do you want to talk about it?" Gigi asked. "It might help you feel better."

The girl nodded. "Uncle Thomas told us they had been traveling on a road that had many curves. A dog darted in front of their carriage from somewhere in the countryside."

"Oh, no." Gigi glanced at the younger girl, who had a trace of tears in her eyes.

Penny nodded. "He said the driver swerved. The horses spooked, though. The driver fell off the box, then the horse ran away with the carriage." A waver sounded in her voice. "It crashed into some trees at the side of the road."

"I can imagine what happened next. You needn't tell me."

The girl's chin trembled. "It is just a story now. Mama and Papa died straightaway. Grandmother died later from the wounds. Grandfather died shortly after returning home." She was such a mature young lady, far older than her years as she told the succinct story.

Gigi's heart went out to both of them. "Were you there with them?"

"No." Penny shook her head. She brushed at a tear that had fallen to her cheek. "Me and Lily were too young to go up to London, so we stayed behind in the country."

She didn't have the heart to correct the grammar. "I'm so sorry."

The girl sniffled. "I wanted to tell Mama goodbye, but I never saw her again."

"Alive?"

"Ever." She shook her head. "Uncle Thomas wouldn't let me see her or them."

"Ah." No doubt he felt the bodies were too battered and bloody for two small girls to look upon, but in doing that, there had been no firm closure.

"Miss Hasting?" Lily crawled close to Gigi.

"Yes?"

"Do you think they hurt before they died?" Sadness flooded the little girl's green eyes.

"Uh…" What to tell her? She didn't want to lie, for life would teach them enough. "Since it was an accident, I am not certain, but you can be sure that God kept them from the worst of it."

I hope.

Penny put her lemonade bottle back in the basket before she too crawled over to Gigi's location. "Do you think they were afraid?"

These were deep questions she had no answers to either, but the girls stared at her with expectation, and she couldn't let them down. "I believe your parents were not afraid. They were with each other, so that made them very happy, and I also believe that whatever happened, it was swift, so there was no time for fear. In fact, your father probably hugged your mother in comfort." At least she liked to hope that had been true.

Except Lily seemed far too upset, so Gigi took the smaller girl into her lap.

"Do you think they thought about us in those moments, Miss Hasting?"

"I…" Gigi swallowed hard. "I'm certain of it. Who wouldn't think about two little girls they loved to the moon and back?" Perhaps her frivolous life hadn't served her as well as it probably should have. Why did she ever think she was qualified enough to be a governess? For the first time, she realized the responsibilities therein were quite large. "If you like, you can both tell them goodbye right now."

Penny frowned. "How? Uncle Thomas says they are buried in a churchyard."

The vicar needed to have lessons in tact.

"Well, in some cultures around the world, there are memorial ceremonies where loved ones are remembered each year, sometimes by putting flowers and wreathes in the water and watching the waves carry them away. It's peaceful and meaningful." She held Lily close. "When you lay the wreath or flowers into the water, you say a prayer or simply talk to your departed loved one. It's best to remember good times you had with them, remember what their laughter sounds like, how their eyes looked when they smiled." When her voice wavered, she cleared her throat. "In that way, you keep them close to your heart."

Lily's eyes rounded. "Can we talk to them whenever we want?"

"Of course." Gigi flashed her a grin. "Think of it like talking to God. You say prayers, correct?" Both girls nodded. "Then this is the same concept. Your parents will always watch over you, and I know they would both be very proud of the young ladies you will grow to be."

Penny tugged on one of Gigi's hands. "Might we put our wreaths in the pond?"

"That is a fine idea." No sooner had they reached the water's edge than the pair of geese followed them over. The swan was quite interested in the flowers, for it kept nipping at the blooms, much to the delight and chagrin of the little girls. "If this keeps up, we might have to invite our feathered friends into the schoolroom."

"We can't do that, Miss Hasting! They will poop on the floor!" A string of giggles followed Lily's statement.

"No, I don't suppose we can." The longer she watched the flower crowns floating on the pond's surface, the more maudlin she grew. Her father would no doubt die soon from his deteriorating faculties, and her mother's health grew more frail with each passing month, no doubt from worrying over her father.

What will I do once Papa dies?

It hadn't been well done of her to treat her father with haughty annoyance over his missteps that had led to the unpaid taxes, especially when he didn't have much time left. Emotion rose in her throat. For the first time since her sisters were forced to take paying positions, she let herself feel the emotions she'd been hiding from.

"Everything is just a mess," she whispered to herself. Though it was embarrassing, she began to cry. "I am not ready to lose my father."

"Are you well, Miss Hasting?" Penny asked with slight alarm in her eyes.

"More or less." But she was glad for the support when both girls gave her quick hugs. "Perhaps we should gather our things and head home." It wasn't good to show such emotion, and if she didn't regain control, she'd become a watering pot in front of her charges. "It's nearly time for tea, regardless. Your uncle is expecting us."

At least seeing him would cheer her.

DEAR HEAVENS, HE smells so good.

Like a mix of clover and how the meadow grass smelled just after a rain and something unidentifiable but delicious that had awareness of the vicar racing over her skin. When she glanced at him from over the rim of her teacup, he grinned, and the gesture danced in his gray eyes. Heat twisted down her spine, and she couldn't help but return the smile.

"I'm glad the three of you had a lovely time this afternoon," he said with a look that encompassed both her and the girls. "It isn't exactly Godly of me, but I find myself envious of that. While you were soaking in the sunshine and enjoying a picnic lunch, I was inside having countless meetings with the poor in the area."

"Everyone has a place in the world, Mr. Alderman. No one is more important than another," Gigi said, and followed it up with a sip of tea.

"Agreed. It takes many hearts to do the Lord's work, to bring comfort to those who have none." He nodded. "I feel the girls will learn much from your lead."

"I'm not sure about that." Though heat filled her cheeks. The praise was unexpected and provoked a smile. She let the girls chatter on to him, feeding him little snippets of how they had spent their day, and when it became obvious they were drooping, she set her teacup in its saucer and laid them both on the low table. "Come, girls. I think you are due for some quiet time."

"What does that mean?" Penny wanted to know. She'd long ago finished her repast.

"It means for the next hour, you are to stay in your room. You can play with your toys, take a nap, sit quietly and draw—whatever you wish—but it's time to rest your minds and your bodies. It's something that is important to practice now, for you will need it as you grow." Standing, she encompassed them both in her gaze. "After that, you'll feel refreshed for your last lesson of the day—painting."

A half hour later, Gigi returned to the parlor where the vicar was finishing up his second cup of tea while reading a copy of *The Times* that was at least a week old.

He glanced up, folded the paper, and then set it down. "Are the girls settled?"

"They are." She perched on the chair she'd vacated before. It sat near enough to his position that she could enjoy his presence without needing to steal glances. "It is something I'm adamant about. Just because they are children doesn't mean they don't deserve time to themselves at some point in the day."

"I envy them. Even an hour to myself each day would be welcome, and a nap, certainly." His chuckle sent shivers along her spine. "Now, since you needn't be strong in front of them, tell me why you are so sad just now."

"What?" When he remained silent with a raised eyebrow, she asked, "How do you know I am?"

"It's easy enough. Your eyes don't sparkle." As he shrugged, embarrassment went through his expression. "Though I do not know you well, I *am* a vicar. It is part of my training to discern the moods of the people in my flock."

"Flock." A giggle that could become hysterical if she wasn't careful escaped Gigi's throat, and she felt much like Lily. "Interesting you chose that word."

His sensuous lips tugged downward with a frown. "I don't understand."

"I had a bit of a to-do with some birds this afternoon, where a pair of geese and a swan took a liking to me." As briefly as she could, she told him what happened during the picnic, but she doubted he believed her, for he looked at her with confusion in his eyes.

"You are upset over waterfowl?"

"Not at all." Another giggle left her throat then she wiped at her eyes that had teared again. "I suppose I'm upset over my father's health. You see, the girls told me about their parents this afternoon, and how they missed them. There were also a few questions."

"Ah. They are young yet; I didn't anticipate it would be difficult."

"It is, and a delicate situation yet, but we worked through it." She told him about the flower crowns and the pond. "I hope you don't mind that I'm teaching them about other cultures. It is something I find fascinating, and I read about such things every chance I have." With a small shrug, she grinned. "You might think me spoiled or too outspoken, but every now and again, I like to feel there are things beyond my ken that learning about will make me… better. That I need to believe there is something bigger than me out there."

That was something she'd never admitted to anyone before,

for fear her parents would lecture and tell her it wasn't something a proper lady should do.

"While that is a lovely sentiment, you haven't told me why you are sad." Compassion reflected in his eyes. "And no. I don't mind you are teaching the girls such things. The world is indeed larger than what they'll experience in England."

She nodded and then sighed. "Suffice it to say, my home situation is constantly changing, Mr. Alderman."

"I think it is perfectly acceptable when we are alone if you refer to me as Thomas."

"Oh!" What an unexpected boon. "Then you may refer to me as Genevieve, or Gigi if you'd rather." She pressed her lips together, and flutters went through her belly when his gaze briefly dropped to her mouth. "My father's mind is rapidly leaving him. Because of worry, my mother is growing weaker. I expect that soon he'll leave us." Emotion rose in her throat. "I should drop by and visit them, to tell them how this first week has gone. Perhaps on Sunday afternoon." It was her one day off each week.

"I would be happy to go with you, to meet with them as well. Offer spiritual comfort if I can." There was no ulterior motive in his voice or attitude.

"Thank you." For long moments, she clasped her hands in her lap. "I suppose I don't enjoy change. I don't want anything to happen to my parents or my family, and when my two older sisters left, that change was inevitable. It is still happening now that they've married."

"Do you resent them for that?"

"For finding love?

"Of course not." She frowned. "But I am a bit annoyed they're out living their lives while the rest of us are here, stuck in the country, while Mama and Papa march toward the grave." Knowing that made her seem unfeeling, Gigi quickly rushed onward. "I don't begrudge them the love or the husbands; all of that is fine enough in its place, but I do resent their freedom."

To a point. After all, they *were* married.

"That is understandable." Thomas nodded. "None of us can avoid change. It is how we grow and mature. How we move from one waypoint in life to the next." The sound of his voice was as comforting as a favorite blanket. "It was difficult for me when I lost four family members at the same time."

"I imagine that was a horrid shock; there was no warning like there is with my parents."

"Indeed. I'm a fourth child and you are a third. There was always someone else responsible for things so we wouldn't need to dirty our hands in them." He rubbed a hand along the side of his face. "Now I've taken on this huge responsibility of having children. Honestly, I don't believe I will be a good father figure for them."

"Why not? They adore you."

He shrugged. "It isn't something I ever thought I would have in my life. I live in terror I won't raise them right, and then someone will blame me."

"Ah." Gigi offered him a genuine smile. "Thus the reason you don't want them to become hoydens."

"Among other things." When he grinned, butterflies danced through her belly.

"Then you hired the wrong woman for a governess. There are a few escapades in my past that would put heat in your cheeks."

"Ha! You sound much like me. I sowed many wild oats in my day." His eyes sparkled with remembered mischief. "I was quite the rogue since there weren't expectations for me."

In that moment, they understood much about each other without needing to speak of it. "I suppose we both need to mature, and frankly, you have already done so. The difference being, I don't want to."

"Oh, I don't know about that. Sooner or later, responsibilities come at us, and we can't avoid them."

"I suppose." With a sigh, Gigi let herself sink into a glum

mood. "It's a bit frightening."

"Perhaps life is supposed to be."

She frowned. "Why? I thought you, as a man of the cloth, would want everything pleasing and ensconced in happiness."

"Perhaps some churches might teach that, but I am also realistic." That grin would soon be her downfall. "If we were always content, we would never grow or change, and both are vital to our futures." When he leaned forward, Thomas rested his forearms on his knees and clasped his hands. "Every life has seasons, and within those seasons, there are sparkling jewels of experiences both good and bad. We cannot enjoy one without the other to temper it."

That made sense. "I'm feeling... restless. Have been for the last several months, and I don't know why."

"It is because you are preparing for change."

That thought made her giggle. "Like a caterpillar into a butterfly?"

"Indeed. You can teach the girls biology. Another positive." Again, he grinned, and she almost vibrated off her chair with need.

"I'm not all that strong on the squishy bits or how flowers reproduce."

"There is plenty of time to learn, hmm?" When he laughed, gooseflesh chased over her skin. "Don't worry over the future, Genevieve. It will come soon enough, whether we are ready for it or not."

"That is exactly what I'm afraid of." Needing something to do, Gigi pushed to her feet. He scrambled to his. "You are calm about this because of fate."

"Or God's plan, however your perspective on that is." Thomas shrugged. "Live in the present. Make an impression and memories. Do the most good that you can. Every step will help you grow."

It was both comforting and confusing to speak with him. "What if I'm not good enough for a better life? What if *this*," she gestured with a hand to indicate her life, "is all there is for me? This feeling alone even when I'm with people?" Never had she admitted to anyone before. It felt… freeing.

"Then talk to God about it. Talk to me about it. I'll try to help, but I'm not perfect either."

For long moments, Gigi stared at him before she nodded. "There is something to be said for finding the imperfections in life." But his looks were not one of them, for he was utter perfection, as if the Creator had spent extra time with him. And then she couldn't help it. She closed the distance, laid a hand on his cheek, threw commonsense to the wind. With a smile, she lifted onto her toes and fit her lips to his.

Shock immediately filled his expression. The dear vicar stood stock still with wide eyes as he watched her with at least a hand's width of space between them.

Oh, I shouldn't have done that. Gigi pulled away. "I apologize. I don't know what I was thinking in kissing you."

"No harm done." His eyes darkened, and a wicked gleam appeared deep in the depths. "In fact, it was rather pleasant. Enough to warrant further research." Thomas put a hand to the small of her back, tugged her closer, and then claimed her lips with his.

A heady rush came over her, and as he introduced himself to her through kisses, Gigi slipped her palms up his chest to hold his shoulders as she matched his overtures. Each movement over her mouth was like a symphony. His lips were both soft but firm, and more to the point, he certainly knew how to kiss to leave the most impact. Within the embrace, possibilities lingered, and suddenly the idea of seducing him was closer than she'd thought. Every second she was in his arms was simply… glorious.

What a waste he'd gone to the Church instead of remaining a rogue, except if he hadn't come to the country, she would never have met him, or never would have discovered how delicious this man truly was.

When something crashed against the floor upstairs, they

sprang apart. Breathless, Gigi stared at him with heat in her cheeks and her heartbeat racing. "Uh… I'd better check on the girls."

"Right." He nodded as ruddy color rose up his neck above his collar. "I have a sermon to finish."

Not knowing what else to do, Gigi ran from the room, and as she gained the staircase, she grinned. Oh, but she wasn't nearly finished with *him*, for that kiss simply hadn't been enough. It woke something prowly and hungry within her that she wanted to explore.

Would he be willing to pursue scandal with her? That remained to be seen, and she couldn't wait to start.

CHAPTER SIX

July 26, 1817
Hawthorn Cottage

THOMAS GLANCED UP as a knock sounded on his partially open study door. And damn if his pulse didn't leap when Genevieve stood there, gently pushing the wooden panel. "Ah, Miss Hasting, what a pleasant surprise. Please, come in."

Dear Lord, it had been a couple of days since they'd shared a fairly chaste kiss. Though there had been enough heat contained in that one meeting of mouths, neither of them had deepened the connection, but it had been seared into his consciousness.

And there was no chance of him forgetting it. Hell, he'd berated himself and then asked God's forgiveness after the fact, for she was absolutely not the sort of woman he needed by his side for the rest of his life, and he wasn't the sort of man who indulged in quick, mad trysts.

"Thank you." When she entered the small space, the faint scent of lilies of the valley carried to his nose. "The girls and I are going out for a walk. You should accompany us."

As she spoke, Thomas focused on her lips and remembered how pillowy soft and supple they were when they'd cradled his, and how much he'd wanted to explore her body—even through clothing—but had been horrified by his response now that he was a man representing the Church. In fact, he hadn't been with a woman since he'd taken the living here.

"Mr. Alderman?" Concern and perhaps a trace of annoyance wove through her voice.

"I beg your pardon. Woolgathering, I suppose." What a nodcock he was. "What did you ask me?"

"If you would like to come walking with the girls and me." Her dress of rose-colored cotton featured daises embroidered along the hem and the rounded bodice, making her look like summer personified.

"It's Saturday, and I haven't yet finished writing my sermon for tomorrow." That hint of cold disappointment in his chest surprised him.

Genevieve pouted. "There is more to life than writing sermons, preparing for them, and delivering them." She propped her hands on her hips, and all he could think about was what a lovely figure she possessed, that she should have been snapped up by any number of men. "Come walking with us. At least to have some exercise. Perhaps your sermon will benefit from some fresh air."

"What of the girls' lessons?"

She shrugged. "We keep modified hours on Saturday, and with the walk, we can collect specimens from nature to study later."

"I don't know. This does need finishing." Thomas tapped his paper with a forefinger.

"And you will do so in good time." When she came closer to his desk, he swore he felt the heat of her. "Besides, if you are truly their guardian, you should spend time with them outside of your vicar capacity. Don't neglect your nieces for the sake of the Church. It is not more important than those you love."

Hmm, well, she did have a point, even if she might not be quite clear on the importance of the Church in his life. Slowly, he nodded. "Perhaps you are correct." With a sigh, he closed the

Bible resting on his desk. "Fresh air does sound lovely." Especially if she were out there enjoying it with him.

The governess smiled. "Good. I'm glad you still retain a bit of common sense about you."

With a start, he realized Genevieve was a boon for the household. "Are you saying I left that behind when I took this position?" As he spoke, Thomas rose to his feet.

She shrugged. "Perhaps I'm implying it." One of her eyebrows rose in question. "Do you deny it?"

"I am not certain." Why did this one woman have the power to confuse him? "To be fair, I don't know how much common sense I had in my days of being a rogue."

"I won't belabor the point since both times in your life you were blindly following someone else's ideals of how you should live." Then she moved to the door. "On the one hand, you thought that by chasing women and vices, you would be accepted by the *ton* and perhaps find meaning, while on the other hand, you now believe that by following arbitrary rules of the Church and removing all interesting bits of yourself, you will be accepted by those you wish to listen to you."

With a frown, he followed her. "I'm not sure it's as black and white as all that."

"Oh, but it is. Perhaps you need to ask yourself why it is you feel this driving need to be accepted at all instead of being confident in who you already are." She glanced over her shoulder at him. "What is it you truly seek?"

"I suppose I need to think about it." But wouldn't a man of the cloth already know the answer to that question? More to the point, wouldn't he have said the love of God was what he sought and sharing that love was above everything else?

Have I failed at this position?

Again?

There was no time to think too much about it, for his nieces exclaimed with surprise the second he and Genevieve stepped into the rear garden.

"Uncle Thomas! Are you joining us?" Penny wanted to know as she rushed over and grabbed his hand.

"Indeed, I am. Miss Hasting convinced me that I should." When he glanced at the governess, her attention was on Lily, whose half-boot had come loose, so she'd kneeled before the child to take care of the issue. Something about that caring gesture tugged at his chest. "Every person should enjoy the outside world and breathe in the country air."

Finally, she looked up, met his gaze, and smiled. "I agree." As she stood, she took Lily's hand. "Where shall we walk today?"

Penny didn't hesitate in answering. "To the pond so Uncle Thomas can see it!" Then she giggled. "And the geese."

Her sister was quite enthused with that plan as well.

Thomas couldn't help his own grin. "Then we should head toward the pond. But only if the two of you practice walking like little ladies."

Giggles erupted from the girls, but they quickly agreed.

The trip was pleasant enough with the sun shining down, the birds singing in the trees, bees and insects buzzing in the flowers, and a beautiful blue sky dotted with fluffy clouds. And the opportunity to spend time with his nieces when he didn't constantly need to correct their behavior or ask them to lower their voices was priceless, yet the jewel of the day was walking beside the unlikely governess who had brought her own brand of sunshine into their lives.

The promise of walking with decorum only lasted a whole two minutes, but he truly didn't mind. One didn't always need to be proper, especially when exercise was required. As they walked, the girls talked of inconsequential things and kept up a stream of conversation between him and Genevieve. It was a pleasant enough sound in their little voices, and surprisingly, he was caught up on their week, being let into their triumphs and tragedies. Through no fault of his own, he realized he'd missed much of their lives while he'd been busy tending to the needs of his parishioners, and that prompted a stab of guilt through his chest.

I must try better to be present in their lives.

Once they arrived at a small pond, the girls' excitement level expanded exponentially. Both of them clamored to show him all their favorite things they'd previous found from other visits to the body of water.

"And look, Uncle Thomas, there are the geese that have fallen in love with Miss Hasting," Penny said as she gestured to the pair of brown geese who were slowly sauntering toward their party. She giggled. "Miss Hasting has geese."

"And a swan!" Lily added with giggles of her own. "A big one!"

"How interesting," Thomas said as he kept one eye on the geese and the other on the governess. "You haven't told me about this development."

A faint blush stained Genevieve's cheeks. "I didn't think it was worth a mention."

"Of course it is!" He grinned as the geese approached her location while the girls went to the edge of the pond, presumably to search for toads. "It speaks to your character that animals feel comfortable in your presence."

"It's rather more annoying than anything else." As she spoke, the geese arrived at her side, bobbing their heads and leaning forward so she could stroke their necks. "The first time we visited the pond, I guess they decided I belonged to them."

"It's adorable and quite humorous." Thomas couldn't help but grin, for it was easily the most pastoral scene he'd ever witnessed. "I suppose if the governess position doesn't last, you could always drive geese about the countryside."

"Bite your tongue, Mr. Alderman."

Suddenly, he wanted to hear his name in her voice. "I believe I asked you to call me Thomas when we are alone."

Mischief sparkled in her eyes as she tried to prevent the geese from nipping at the fabric of her dress. "Are we alone enough for all of that... Thomas?"

Dear heavens, how wonderful was that? In her dulcet tones, it was almost as if she flirted with the words before she finally released them into the air.

With a glance at the girls who ran along the edge of the pond, he nodded. "I believe that we are." When he met her gaze again, awareness prickled along his skin. "How have you enjoyed your first week as a governess?"

"It has been quite an interesting endeavor, but the girls are sweet. Our friendship is coming along nicely." A slight smile curved her lips. "I never thought I would like taking a paid position, but this isn't as bad as I thought it might be."

"I'm impressed you've committed to taking on the twin dervishes there. Before you came along, I hadn't luck in even getting some of the women past the interview process." As they strolled toward the girls and the pond, the geese escorted them. Soft honks issued from the birds as if they were completely satisfied with their life.

"I suppose none of those women would have fit as well in the position because a firm constitution and hand is needed with your nieces." Genevieve smiled as Penny turned around and looked at them. "They are young yet, but they are learning."

"I look forward to further settling into the new schedule of things." There was no time to say more, for Penny tugged at his hand.

"May Lily and I swim?" She looked at him with those big green eyes and his heart threatened to melt. How could he deny her?

"Uh…" It wasn't exactly a proper activity.

Genevieve nudged his shoulder with hers, and electric sensation coursed down his arm. "Who will see them in the middle of rural rolling hills and meadows?"

"True, and we won't abandon them."

"Of course not. What sort of uncle would that make you, or what sort of governess would I be in that instance?" Another twinkle of mischief glimmered in the blue depths of her eyes. He turned his attention to Penny. "You and your sister may splash about as much as you like, but don't go too far from either of us."

When Genevieve sank onto the grass and folded her legs beneath her, she gestured at the girls. "Come here. No need to dirty your dresses." Then she effortlessly stripped both girls down to their shifts and petticoats. "Be mindful of each other. Your sister is your responsibility, Penny, because she is younger than you."

"All right." Though Penny didn't sound excited about the prospect, she took Lily's hand and then both girls waded into the shallow water of the pond.

With nothing else to do, and feeling slightly awkward standing next to her, Thomas sank to the grass beside the governess. The temperature while in the full sunshine was quite warm, and as much as he wished to remove his jacket, he didn't dare in front of Genevieve. That was far too scandalous and not the sort of behavior a vicar should exhibit.

"Truly, I have never seen the girls as happy as they are right now. This past year has been difficult on all of us." Perhaps life moved on, or perhaps it was Genevieve's influence and calming presence, but it was much appreciated. "So thank you for that."

"It was my pleasure. They aren't bad or horrid. They are merely lost, I think, but it's good they have you." Never did she take her eyes off her young charges. The giggles and laughter from the girls filtered back to their location. "Though you might have your hands full when they get older."

"There is that, but I shall worry about it when I meet said challenge." Wiping the sweat from his brow, he grinned when Lily squealed. Penny had just splashed water onto the other girl. "I didn't anticipate how difficult it would be to go from an unrepentant rogue to a proper vicar."

"No one said you needed to be one or the other, Thomas." Amusement threaded through Genevieve's voice. She glanced at him, and the same sentiment slightly curved her lips... lips he wouldn't mind kissing again, and longer this time, to further introduce himself to her. "They are both examples of what a man can be, but there is no rule that says a vicar cannot enjoy himself if the occasion demands."

"As much as I want to believe you, I'm afraid I must follow the dictates of the Church as well as the guide map the Bible provides."

She huffed, apparently in annoyance. "The Church is guided by a man. Not by God or any other deity, but by a man, and vicars all over England are merely following that *man's* opinions." Briefly glancing away from the girls, she rested the full force of her gaze on him. "You are quite capable of forming your own opinions about what the Bible says or doesn't, as the case usually is." A shrug lifted one shoulder but drew his interest to the lace-edged bodice and the swell of her modest breasts. "Haven't you learned by now that the men in charge of any church are quite skilled in controlling the population out of fear?"

"I did hear a few grumbles about that while attending seminary."

"Ah, then if learned men intent on being vicars talk about the same thing that a woman of the *ton* has been able to work out on her own, there must be some weight in it." Again, she shrugged. "But then, men need to make their own decisions. I'm afraid I cannot abide weak-willed men who follow another's dictates because someone somewhere said he *should*."

How very interesting. "Have you always been this outspoken?"

"Yes." Her attempt at stifling a giggle failed. "I have found it saves time as well as wards off misunderstandings. Additionally, I don't believe that women should be subservient to anyone. Respectful, surely, but only if I have also been shown the same."

"What are your hopes for the future?" The woman was beyond fascinating. "Do you intend to marry eventually? You surely cannot be so old as to put yourself on the shelf already."

"I am seven and twenty, not ancient." With the toss of her head, he was given a glimpse of her slender neck and the curve of her jaw, enhanced by the ribbons of her bonnet. "Though I do give it much thought each time my mother opens this conversation, I maintain that if I wish to marry, the man must have a title as well as copious amounts of coin. Since I am struggling now with my family, scrimping and saving for every little thing, I do not want to do that in my married life or for the rest of my existence."

"That is understandable." After crooking his knees, he rested his wrists atop them. "Women are treated much differently in our society and there is not much available to them outside of marriage." No doubt they would wish to be financially taken care of as well. "Does that mean you don't believe one should marry for love?"

For the space of a few heartbeats, Genevieve remained silent. "While love might suit others, I rather doubt that is something I would be interested in."

Of all the things he expected to hear from her, that wasn't it. "What do you mean? Everyone should strive to find love at least once in their life."

"Perhaps." She frowned as she watched the girls cavort in the water. "While my parents have enjoyed a lovely marriage and are no doubt still captivated by each other, I cannot help but wonder how that union held up when the hard times came. Any moment we expect the letter that will say the manor house will be taken away due to unpaid taxes, and Papa's health is rapidly declining." When she turned her face to him and met his gaze, both sadness and a trace of panic reflected there. "I am not certain I have the strength to survive such hardships. My mother is a true brick, but I am not her."

"Then you feel that everything in life shouldn't challenge us and should prove easy, that we shouldn't strive to overcome anything and gain satisfaction because of it?" Honestly, he didn't know how to respond.

"That is exactly it. I don't know. About any of it. Life remains much a mystery, which is essentially change, and that terrifies me." With a sigh, she again looked at him. "Regardless, I do hope to marry eventually, but the man who I do marry must not expect me to be a proper *ton* lady who will wear a bonnet all the time or even stays. That is just who I am."

And that, perhaps more than her wish to marry a titled man with coin to his name, would leave her out of the running for a helpmeet on his part. A man who was a vicar could ill-afford wedding a woman who simply wasn't proper or someone the Church would accept.

Not that he had such designs on her.

"Well, thank you for telling me that. It's an interesting insight into your life, and I'm certain those admissions were difficult for you." Above all, he appreciated that she was honest about it. Too many women claimed to want one thing but accepted something completely different. "I'm afraid I have no lofty expectations. I merely wish to find someone I get on well enough with that holds the same values and mindset that I do who might wish to give back to the community by working in the church in some capacity."

"Wouldn't marrying a woman who thinks and acts the same way that you do grow incredibly dull after a time?" After fussing with the ribbons beneath her chin, Genevieve finally tugs at the ends, and then removed the bonnet completely. In many ways, it was a sign that she trusted him and was letting him into her private world. "There would be no opposition, no difference of opinion, no viewpoints in which to see things in a new light. How dull your life would grow after a few years."

Point taken. "Or would it simply be a breath of fresh air to know there would be no arguments?"

"Only you can decide that, but as for me, I would welcome the chance to cross swords with a man, to go toe-to-toe with him knowing he wouldn't respond with weakness and give into me just because I could bully him." Nothing except honesty shone from her eyes. "And wouldn't making amends and apologies prove quite exciting afterward?"

Well, she would certainly keep someone on their toes. "I hope you find exactly what you search for, Genevieve. You deserve at least that."

"As do you, Thomas."

They sat side by side in the grass for a long time after that discussion, and no other attempt at words was made for some time.

Eventually, she stood with her bonnet in hand. "It is no doubt time for tea, and I'm a bit famished. Being in this heat simply makes me wilt." Before he could say anything in response, she moved through the grasses toward the pond. The two geese joyfully paddled over to meet her at the edge, where she called the girls to order and asked them to don their clothing once more.

When protests started, Genevieve wasn't having any of it, and in short order, she had the girls both garbed in their dresses, stockings, and half boots. It was quite an impressive feat.

Penny brightened as she submitted to the governess's ministrations of tying the bonnet ribbons beneath her chin. "Hey Lily, I'll race you to the main road. Winner gets to pick a treat from the tea tray first!" Then she was off like a shot.

"No fair! You have longer legs!" But what Lily might lack in height, she gained in speed. So much so that her bonnet fell to her back, only held onto her person by the ribbons. In moments, they had dashed up the hill and left the adults still walking through the meadow.

"One would think swimming should have made them tired," Thomas groused as the sun beat down on him and sweat trickled along his spine.

Genevieve snorted. "They are always like that until it's time for bed. Which is exactly why I encourage them to have an hour of quiet time following tea. It's as much for me as it is them." She fanned her face with a hand. "This summer has turned quite steamy. I hope the heat doesn't last very long."

"Nothing trying will ever test our patience for longer than we can endure." It sounded trite in that moment, for he would do anything to turn tail and run fully clothed into that pond merely to cool his overheated skin. "We haven't had rain for a spell, which makes everything that much worse." And worse than that was the fact that he couldn't seem to stop looking at her mouth or stop wanting to kiss those lips again.

Pull yourself together, man! You are a leader of the Church, not a skirt-chasing rogue any longer.

A sigh escaped her throat. "To be honest, I wouldn't have minded swimming myself, but obviously I couldn't do that in mixed company or while my employer watched. I might not be proper and don't believe one should always observe propriety, but I don't want the girls to think such behavior is encouraged."

Damn, but the woman was a delightful mix of contrasts. "I wouldn't have minded taking a dip either, but most men swim in the nude." Why had he said that? To tease her?

"Ah." Genevieve's eyes rounded while a pink flush went through her cheeks. "I wonder if you are hiding an impressive figure behind those somber clothes, Vicar."

There was only so much willpower a man possessed. Despite her teasing and worldly attitude, he was sure she was an innocent. And it was far too tempting. Both heaven and hell in one petite package. "I guess neither of us shall know, for you won't see it and I won't indulge your curiosity." After checking that the girls were nowhere around, and knowing he and the governess hadn't yet crested the hill to be observed, he tossed common sense away, took Gigi into his arms, and set out to properly kiss her this time. With a half-stifled groan, he wrapped his arms around her until she was settled comfortably in that embrace.

Briefly, she pulled away to peer into his eyes. "You are all too potent. What a lovely surprise for a vicar." She drew in a shuddering breath before she kissed him back, mimicking every subtle movement and overture he made toward her then seconds later, she began a campaign of kissing him on her own.

And he was nearly lost.

Hot desire circled through him while over and over Thomas claimed her mouth. He couldn't have enough. Her lips were warm from the sun, and they cradled his with soft perfection. As he roved his hands along her back, he thrilled at her taste, her touch; her warmth consumed him. When he found the sweet curve of her arse, he squeezed, hauling her upward so that he could press her against his burgeoning arousal. Could she feel how she excited him? Did she want him as much as he wanted her? The questions sank beneath the fog of passion as he encouraged her lips apart and touched his tongue to hers.

"Why, Mr. Alderman, what a naughty man you are. It would seem old habits are difficult to break," she said against his lips, and hers brushed his with every word. The hand resting on his chest circled into his lapel and a gentle but insistent tug at his nape had him kissing her once more.

They warred for dominance as satin slid across silk and tongues thrust or parried depending on the need. Already neck deep into sinning, Thomas trailed a hand down her arm, the skin sun-warmed and soft, and then he dared to cup one of her breasts, for she was already pressed quite intimately against his form.

A barely audible moan escaped her, and he grinned, went so far as to worry the nipple into a hard, tight bud before dropping his hand and pulling slowly away from her. Those kiss-swollen lips of hers formed a pout. Her eyes had darkened to sapphires. "Why did you stop?"

"Because if I didn't, I'm afraid this wouldn't have ended with a mere kiss or a touch." At least it was honest. "We should catch up with the girls else they'll grow suspicious."

"Well, it wouldn't be the only something… growing." With obvious relish, Genevieve slid her gaze down the front of his person to linger at the obvious bulge in the front of his breeches before bringing her regard back up to his face. "Give yourself a few minutes then come join us." Then she winked and climbed the rest of the way to the crest of the gentle hill.

When he was able to, Thomas caught up to them when they gained the road, just as Penny's trills of laughter rang in his ears.

"Miss Hasting, you must be hot from the sun because your cheeks are red."

And both girls laughed.

"I suppose that must be it," she said while looking over their heads and finding his gaze. "After all, what could possibly make a woman more heated than that?"

Well, damn it all. And he didn't even mind the vulgarity. *I'm in trouble.* The old yearnings flared again, and he wouldn't be able to resume his placid, God-fearing life again until he'd bedded the damned governess. But he couldn't. It was against everything he believed in now.

Wasn't it?

Perhaps he needed to spend more time on his knees seeking God's counsel… or permission. And if that didn't work, forgiveness, for that was always easier after the sin.

CHAPTER SEVEN

July 28, 1817

"**G**O OUTSIDE AND play in the garden. I shall join you in a few minutes for our lesson on native plant life," Gigi said to the girls as they finished their luncheon in the attic room that had been set aside for schoolwork. Any time after the meal, she refused to use the attic space, for it was much too warm in the summer.

"Can we dig for worms?" Penny wanted to know as she bounded off her chair.

"I would rather you didn't since we have an afternoon of lessons to attend." When the girl groaned, she held up a hand. "However, if we get through the lessons early, then you may dig for worms after tea."

Lily was much slower to leave the table, for if there was one thing she adored doing, it was eating. "Could we pick flowers?"

"Not from the bushes in your uncle's garden. I believe those are for the tea table and dinner table, but if you find some wildflowers close by, then by all means build your own bouquet."

"For you?" the little girl wanted to know.

"Only if you wish it." Gigi gathered the used dishes to make it easier on the maid when she came to clean up.

Penny came close with a particular sparkle in her green eyes. "Have you ever received one from a man?"

"A few times."

Lily giggled. "From Uncle Thomas?"

Heat built in Gigi's cheeks as she remembered that kiss from that day at the pond. "Of course not. I'm your governess, not someone he is courting."

"Oh." Penny frowned. "Why can he not give you flowers anyway?"

"It's not proper, and remember, it is my responsibility to teach you what is proper and what isn't." Too much more time spent in this conversation, and she would be in the weeds. Finished at the table, she stood and shooed the girls toward the door. "If you linger too long here, I'll give you an extra lesson."

"No!" Penny was almost feral in her denial of more learning.

As if those were magic words, both Penny and Lily pelted from the room and down the narrow wooden stairs. Their footsteps echoed as they gained the second floor and continued down the stairs.

"I can't say that I blame you," Gigi murmured to herself, for she had been much like Penny in her aversion to book learning, which was why she tried to make certain their lessons didn't come from books all that much. Of course, it was the summer yet, and a serious school "term" hadn't yet begun. No doubt all of that would change once autumn arrived.

After she'd tidied the room, she stopped in her tiny bedchamber to freshen up then on the stairs, she met the housekeeper who had folded bed linens in her arms.

"Be advised, Miss Hasting. The vicar has a visitor just now," Mrs. Traverse said with a slight smirk on her face.

"Oh? Who?" While it wasn't rare for Thomas to have visitors, usually *he* called upon various members of his flock.

The older woman shrugged. "A Miss Partridge. If I remember correctly, she's the daughter of a squire, and rumor holds she is quite desperate to marry since she just passed her twenty-third birthday."

"Ah, the terror of becoming an old maid is a good motivator." Gigi winked, for she and the housekeeper had enjoyed a few cuppas with a few snippets of gossip in the week that she'd been installed as a governess.

With a grin, Mrs. Traverse continued on her way up the stairs while Gigi went downward. Because she had no shame and because she was more than a little curious, she crept to the open parlor door and paused in the corridor outside the room merely to listen.

"I hope you enjoy this cake, Vicar. I made it myself, and I'm told my vanilla spice cakes are second to none in the village."

When Gigi peeked her head around the doorframe, her gaze fell on a pretty young lady with clouds of brunette hair and a gorgeous white frosted cake resting on a lovely porcelain platter on the low table. And she was making calf-eyes at Thomas.

"I'm sure it will be a delightful dessert for the girls and me after dinner. Thank you, Miss Patridge, for thinking of us." He was as nice and polite as he was with everyone, but the woman did her level best to flirt with him.

"Oh, it was actually *you* I thought about the whole time I made that cake," she said in a breathless sort of voice. "In fact, I find myself thinking about you *often*."

Gigi moved away from the door so they couldn't see her while she pointed her gaze briefly to the heavens. Could the woman be any more obvious in her attempts?

"I am not sure how to respond to that, Miss Partridge," Thomas said with confusion clear in his voice. "However, I'm glad you came to visit. As I said, we will put this cake to good use."

"Let us forget about the cake for the next few moments." Fabric rustled, indicating the young woman had moved, no doubt to be closer to Thomas. "You work far too much, Vicar Alderman. Why don't you come to the community summer fete that is coming up? It will be held in the village square at the end of the month, and I'm responsible for helping to decorate." When Gigi peeked around the doorframe again, Miss Patridge's eyes shone. "After dinner *alfresco*, they will have dancing. I would very much enjoy sharing a set with you."

"I see."

As Gigi hid once more, she clapped a hand over her mouth to stifle the giggle rising in her throat. Yes, the woman was quite desperate.

"And if you attend the fete, you and I can come to know each other better, for I care about your congregation as much as you do." Fabric rustled again. Perhaps she'd reached out to touch his hand or arm. "You have been quite successful as a vicar and your flock continues to grow. Surely you will need a helpmeet soon."

Gigi's lower jaw hung open. *Cheeky woman!*

"That part of my life is not up for further discussion." Though the answer was non-committal, there was a certain hard edge in his voice. "If there is nothing else, I'll again thank you for the cake. I should return to my work."

Of course, Miss Partridge wouldn't be dismissed so easily. "I understand that, Vicar, but you must understand that gossip is moving through the congregation." Fabric rustled, and when Gigi peeked into the parlor, it was to find that the visitor had stood and approached the chair where Thomas had just scrambled to his feet. "Your nieces need a mother, and this place needs a woman's touch."

Thomas frowned. "I think the decorating has gone rather well."

"Perhaps. However, it's a known fact around the congregation that you are quite a sought-after bachelor. Which makes you, and by association the village, the subject of gossip and rumors."

"Why?" He retreated a few steps. "It is not a crime nor a sin to be unmatched. Nor is it a sin to be the youngest son of a viscount."

"True, but your marital status—or lack thereof—might prove too great a temptation, especially since you have employed a governess for the girls, and one who is not unattractive and one who is still fairly young, if only just."

Thomas huffed. "What difference does any of that make?"

"Perhaps it doesn't, but surely you know how small-minded people in villages are. Rumors can damage a budding career in the Church, don't you think? Who knows where you might go from a country vicar."

The woman was trying to manipulate him on the grounds of ambition! Gigi was affronted on his behalf. *What a minx!* Before she could step into the parlor with a few choice words, Thomas cleared his throat.

"Once more, thank you for coming by and bringing a cake. It was a lovely gesture." His voice growing louder coupled with the tread of footsteps indicated he was drawing near to the door with Miss Patridge trailing him.

With her heartbeat tripping through her veins, Gigi darted across the hall and into the common room while still listening.

"You are quite welcome. I do hope you will attend the fete, Vicar." Warmth and sweetness threaded through Miss Partridge's voice. "The sooner you make a choice, the sooner you enter into an engagement, the more settled everyone will feel. And you can move into the next part of your life."

"Thank you. I shall think over your words and concern. When I choose to court a woman or offer up an engagement, is no one's business except mine."

Then they were in the corridor as Thomas escorted his visitor to the front door.

How bold of Miss Partridge to come here and practically tell him in no uncertain terms if he didn't find someone to wed, rumors would tear his congregation apart! And, of course, she would offer herself up as a good candidate for his wife. Gigi shook her head and bit down on her lower lip. Granted, he was attractive and in good health, and the living he worked at was nothing to sneeze at. Additionally, he was from a titled family, who would no doubt take him in if he decided to leave the

Church.

That was large bait, indeed, if one were fishing.

While Thomas was still at the door, Gigi slipped out of the room and returned to the stairs as quietly as she could. All of that might be true, but he shouldn't have to force a courtship or engagement merely to make others feel more comfortable.

And even more concerning, why did she care who was trying to bedevil the vicar?

BY THE TIME night fell that evening, Gigi couldn't endure the stifling temperatures inside the cottage. She hadn't seen Thomas since tea that afternoon, for he had dinner at the home of one of his parishioners. He'd come home a few hours later but closeted himself into his study.

Perhaps he had paperwork to catch up on.

Once Penny and Lily had drifted off to dreamland, she deemed it safe to sneak away from the cottage. As she left, the carriage-style clock on the mantel in the common room chimed the midnight hour.

Outside, with the nighttime insects buzzing and the nocturnal animal life thrumming all around her, Gigi made her way to the stream that ran along the western side of the property. It was an amazing walk, for she had always been drawn to the night and the moon and stars. The darkness felt comforting, as if someone had put their arms around her and held her in comfort. During the night, her dreams didn't sound silly in those silent hours as they did in the daylight, nor did life seem as hopeless.

What would happen once her father lost his battle with the demons in his brain?

What would happen to the manor if the taxes couldn't be caught up?

What would happen once Thomas truly did take a bride? It

was unlikely she would be able to remain in this position, for the cottage wasn't big enough to hold all those people, and any woman in her right mind would demand a young, progressive governess be sacked immediately.

I cannot think about those things right now.

Her mind obliged, but then it stuck on a different topic altogether. What would happen if she found the titled, rich man she'd always dreamed about and then ultimately married? Could she endure a life of having everything being scheduled and well-ordered, of having responsibilities and expectations even if there were enough coin for leisure? A life of predictability?

Do I want such a life where every day is the same and there are no surprises?

The thought left her cold with unease, and she hurried through the darkness as she clasped the handle of the willow basket. Perhaps it didn't matter what her future held, for she would meet those challenges when they came. Unfortunately, she was growing older and was nearly on the shelf, and at times that didn't sit well.

But what else was there to do? For now, she was a governess. God only knew what she would be in six months.

And when would this heat break? It would drive her mad before too long. At least bathing in the stream would cool her skin, and the light from the full moon would provide another way to bathe. There was something both eerie and healing about the moon's glow set against the midnight-velvet sky strewn with stars. Finally having time to herself and a few moments of silence was much like what heaven would probably feel like.

At the stream, a sigh escaped Gigi's throat. The bubbling, gurling sounds of the stream were the gentlest music and immediately soothed her turbulent thoughts. After setting her willow basket on the bank, it took very little time to strip down to her shift, and with the bank strewn with her discarded clothing, she eased her feet into the cool water.

"Goodness but that is quite refreshing." The barely moving

water tickled her toes and upper calves. Leaning down, she splashed some of the liquid onto her knees and thighs, and another sigh left her. "It's a shame that swimming isn't an activity proper young ladies can do whenever they want without being shielded from a wandering eye."

It took a few moments to find a spot within the stream that was comfortable yet optimized the most of the slow-flowing water, but eventually she sat on a flat rock and moaned as the cool water encompassed her legs, thighs, buttocks, and her lap. The water didn't quite reach her waist, but she didn't care. A few splashes of the wetness cooled her upper body until the lawn shift clung to her body.

Being one with the outside elements, lifting her face to the moon's shine returned the strength and patience to her that she'd lost over the course of the week. This was the beginning of the second one as a governess, and honestly, she didn't know how other women did it, but she adored those two little girls, and hoped they would come out the other side of this with more manners than how she'd found them.

Once soaking up nature paled, she removed a chipped teacup from the basket and used it to soak her hair, for it had been a while since she'd last washed it. The bar of finely milled French soap imparted the subtle aroma of lilacs as she ran it through her wet tresses. It might be vain and silly, but that bar of soap was one of the things she'd brought from home, and it was a precious commodity besides. It had been something she'd tucked away once her father's financial difficulties had come to light; she'd kept it back to pamper herself at a later date. Perhaps that time was now, and she enjoyed every indulgent second of it.

Bathing her skin was the next task, and by the time she finished, her whole body smelled faintly of lilacs. It was one of the best moments in recent memory, and after she'd rinsed the soap from her person, she carefully wrapped the remainder of the bar in its protective paper and replaced it in the basket. Then she brought forth an ivory-handled comb from a set she'd received as a gift on the occasion of her sixteen birthday, which she'd had to hide in the garden when her father had gathered up things he could quickly sell for coin.

As the rhythmic strokes of the comb's teeth went through her mildly tangled hair—which reached her waist—Gigi's mind once more wandered, along with her fingers. She might be seven and twenty and still an innocent, but she'd learned several years ago that when those strong feelings of longing and restlessness came over her, she could easily bring herself back to calm by exploring her own body. After learning about the carnal side of life that went on between men and women by spying on some of the staff, or listening to whispered conversations from her friends who'd lain with men—for her mother certainly hadn't talked to her about such things, and according to her older sisters, that talk wouldn't come until she was nearly wed—she'd figured out how to evoke the hysteria inside herself as well as how to relieve that tension.

Especially when nothing ever resulted from passionate kissing she indulged in with various men around the village or before that when she'd been fortunate to have a few Seasons in London… before life changed and went in a completely different direction.

A few minutes rubbing her fingers over her hardened nipples had those fires building in her blood; the night was perfect for it, and she gave herself over to the growing madness within. Dear heavens, how she adored those breath-catching sensations as if her whole body would be collected into a whirlwind of desire and heat. Over and over, she teased those taut buds, held her breasts in her hands and squeezed, constantly teasing. Only then did she twist and pluck the nipples to increase the pleasurable feelings. Need fluttered through her lower belly, and she welcomed the familiar longing, but just as she slipped one of her hands beneath the hem of her wet shift and between her splayed thighs, the snap of a twig alerted her to the presence of someone else in the area with her.

Frustrated and a bit annoyed, Gigi glanced about the area. "Who's there?" And who would have the gall to spy on a woman?

Then the shadows separated themselves to coalesce into the form of a man—Thomas. He stepped from the wooded cover, and she sucked in a breath, for he wore breeches and a lawn shirt rolled up to his elbows. Another dried twig broke beneath his boot sole as he came closer.

"I apologize for the intrusion, for I only wished to make certain you were safe."

Shock rolled over her to nearly bury the feelings of bliss she'd nearly had before. "You followed me here?"

"Not exactly, but I was restless, and when I went downstairs to put on the kettle, I noticed the door to your room a tiny bit ajar. Upon further inquiry, you weren't inside, and neither were you downstairs, so I figured you'd gone out..."

"And you followed me." She didn't know whether to be angry or grateful. At least she was no longer alone in the night, but she was at a disadvantage, and he hadn't stopped staring at her since he arrived.

"Perhaps. I, uh, heard a moan and thought you might be in peril..." He cleared his throat, his eyes shining in the moonlight. "Which obviously you are not, so I will leave you to your privacy."

Just when he was about to turn, Gigi slowly stood up from the water. She didn't care that her shift still clung to her form or that her hair fell over her shoulders; if he hadn't wished to spy or find her in a compromising position, he should have left well enough alone. "What if I no longer want to be alone?"

"Ah, I..." To his credit, the vicar *did* look away... for all of a few seconds. Soon his regard returned, and he roved his gaze up and down her form as if he hadn't seen a woman so scantily clad before. Her nipples tightened once more as if he'd caressed her with his hands.

Would he be open to a bit of scandal? "Cat got your tongue, Thomas?" She made certain her voice was low, slightly smoky.

Men seemed to respond to that, and she was feeling far too reckless to try and appear proper; in fact, she wanted excitement and daring... and scandal. "I'd much rather have that tongue employed in other, more creative ways if you are of the same mind."

Was that too blatant of an overture? Made her too wanton?

"Dear God," he whispered, and he came forward another few steps until he stood at the bank of the stream near her discarded clothing. "You tempt me, Gigi, so very much, but I am not that man any longer. Can't be."

"Why not?" Desire circled low in her belly. The attraction that had crackled between them since the first moment they'd met demanded satisfaction. "There is nothing wrong with appreciating the female form."

"But I am a man of the cloth now, a vicar..."

"Who has needs just like every other man in existence," she continued as she slipped a hand down the front of her damp shift, grinning when he followed the gesture with his eyes. "Why can you not set aside the face you show to the public for a little bit and indulge in something merely for you? If you still consider it a sin, can you not ask for forgiveness after the fact?" Wasn't that how it worked when one believed in God's love and forgiveness? "Otherwise, you keep yourself from everything good and lovely in this world."

Thomas struggled. He rubbed a hand along the side of his face. "I'm to hold myself above the rest of the world."

She huffed in frustration. "Kissing a woman, regardless of her state of dress, is not a sin and won't send you to hell. Why must you let fear control you? God isn't going to swoop down from the clouds to smite you dead for appreciating a nearly naked woman in a moment of privacy." More annoyed than she'd anticipated, Gigi removed herself from the stream to join him on the bank. "But fine. Do what you must. It matters not to me; except I'll wager becoming a vicar made you weaker in will than when you were merely a viscount's son with nothing to lose." She met his eyes, so bright and nearly silver in the moonlight, and shrugged. "A pity I didn't know you then, for we could have had much fun together."

It wasn't well done of her to say such things, but she wanted that next kiss, to see how far he would go, and if he could quell the rising desire, the wave of loneliness and need battering her, so be it.

Only this one time, then she'd go back to try her hand at being a proper governess.

CHAPTER EIGHT

*H*ELLFIRE AND DAMNATION. That was what waited for him if he called the lady out on her bluff, and she was a huge temptation, in both words and looks. When he'd come upon her, realized that she was bringing herself to pleasure, his world had tilted. He'd only followed her out of the house to lend protection, but this had the potential to become so much more if he weren't careful.

And he couldn't stop staring at her.

In the moonlight, with her golden hair falling down her back and over her shoulders in long damp curls, she was every inch a celestial goddess or a woodland sprite. Clad only in a shift that clung scandalously to every curve she owned, she could easily be a siren of old. The dark pink tips of her hardened nipples showing through the thin fabric nearly had him on his knees, but it was her forthright and daring attitude that captivated him whole and drew him toward her.

"You think I'm somehow less now that I've become a vicar." It wasn't a question.

When she shrugged, the damp fabric pulled taut across her breasts. Interest shivered along his shaft. "I didn't say that, but are you?"

"I would like to believe I am not. However, I've also not been with a woman since I took the position as vicar here." He'd never admitted that to anyone, not even his close friends, for not only was it embarrassing, but it was also slightly puzzling.

One of her eyebrows rose in surprise. "Then you should be well primed, hmm?"

Every word she spoke chipped away at his resolve to remain a gentleman. "Why are you so intent on entering scandal and dragging me with you?"

Genevieve stepped over the grass to him, pausing only when she was a hand's breadth away from him. Her eyes were round and dark in the moonlight, full of the same desire currently slamming through his veins. "What is the point of living if you don't ever do things that remind you that you are truly alive?"

What indeed?

The remainder of his willpower dissolved like sugar in the rain, and with a growl, Thomas tugged her into his arms and at the same time, he claimed her lips in a fierce kiss.

Like the last time they'd come together like this, there was every bit of that odd connection, as if someone had dropped a match to dry tender, only this time that energy was somehow enhanced. Was it due to the fact they were under cover of nightfall, in varying degrees of undress, caught up finally in a wave of passion neither one could deny?

It didn't matter, for in this moment, there was only her and him, and he couldn't deny that he wanted this woman.

Pulling away merely to breathe and perhaps feast his gaze on the delicious picture she made when she wasn't forced to convey a proper image, Thomas grinned. In the shadows of the night, she was more beautiful and alluring than she'd ever been while sharing tea or dinner with him.

"You are leading me on a merry chase, my dear, so where do you want this to end?" he asked in a barely audible voice, even though they were very clearly alone while the nighttime world buzzed and croaked and skittered around them.

"Does it matter?" With a wicked twinkle in her eyes, Genevieve retreated as he advanced, edging more toward a small clearing not far from the stream. "Can I not desire a string of scandalous kisses?"

"Is that what you wish to stop at?" When she didn't answer, merely grinned, he quickly continued. "After all, we *have* been flirting with the fine line between scandal and propriety ever since you took the position to governess."

"Ha. Well, *I* have." She chuckled as he stepped closer, so close the heat from her body seeped into his. "The question now remains: will we step over the line?" Then she plucked at the fine lawn of his loose shirt and pulled him closer. When he slipped his arms around her, she grinned. "Are you brave enough?"

"In this moment? I would say yes." And he would pray for forgiveness later. Needing to touch her, Thomas slipped one of his hands to cup her cheek, but not wanting her to be in control, he yanked her hard against his body… and his length pulsed in agreement. Damn, but it felt good to have a woman in his arms again.

And a willing woman at that.

"That is an encouraging first step."

"Why do I feel you enjoy exchanging verbal swords with me far too much?" When interest flickered through her eyes, he slid a hand down her spine to rest on one of her buttocks. "Shall we move onto the next phase?"

"I will say yes, quite enthusiastically, and if knocks you from that lofty pedestal you've placed yourself on, all the better."

"Ah, Gigi, your thinking is both wrong but refreshing and makes me think deeper." Because he could, and he needed to feel her lips on his, he crushed his mouth to hers in an opening salvo.

With a soft sound of surprise at the back of her throat, she moved her hands up his chest and loosely looped her arms about his shoulders. Then she apparently wanted to kiss him back and make it a memorable embrace.

Well played, my lady.

But he refused to let her boss him during that kiss. Instead, he settled her more comfortably into his embrace, and then he took full command of the kiss, for he wasn't a former rogue for nothing. If she wanted a tryst, he would give her the best of what he knew. Thomas moved over her lips with slow leisure that he hoped would drive her mad. When she applied pressure at his nape in a bid to hurry him along, he ignored her and took his time.

"It would behoove you to learn patience, Miss Hasting," he whispered and then kissed her all the more.

Over and over, he nipped and nibbled her lips. Soft but firm, those two pieces of flesh both cradled his and provided enough stimulation and heat that his body started to vibrate and shift with the wonder of doing anything so intimate.

When he drew the tip of his tongue along her lower lip, she shivered and gasped, held him ever closer. With a smug chuckle, he fenced with her tongue, wishing to make a lasting impression, and one she wouldn't soon forget. Time seemed to slow as they both chased that erotic delight that only kissing in the French style could give, and all too soon he was randy as hell.

Desire clouded his brain as the heady embrace continued. Though it was the middle of summer, he craved her heat, both inside and out. In a matter of seconds their bodies were layered scandalously against each other as they continued to fight for dominance in the embrace. Damn if it wasn't breathtaking, made him regret giving up that sort of life in favor of the Church. The faint floral scent of her accelerated his heartbeat, and he wanted her all the more.

Eventually, he pulled away to drag his lips down the satiny side of her neck while her fingers went into his hair. Then he guided his lips to the tops of her breasts above the plain bodice of her shift while he drew his hands up and down her sides.

"How are you so intoxicating?" he whispered against her skin, and he didn't give her a chance to answer, for he cupped her breasts, teased the nipples through the thin fabric, and every breath she took, every shiver she executed, fired his need.

"I could ask the same of you," she said and licked at the underside of his jaw. "Never before have I been so attracted to anyone connected with the Church."

He should have put a halt to this interlude right then, but he couldn't keep his hands off her body, couldn't bear to relinquish the closeness between them. "Shall I consider myself honored, then?" There was something about the feel and warmth of her modest breasts in his hands, how the hardened nipples demanded his attention, and he was only a man without willpower any longer, so dipped his head and took one of those pebbled tips into his mouth.

"Thomas, yes!" The hiss of approval hovered on the summertime air. Genevieve arched her back, which put her more firmly into his hold, and he couldn't be more thrilled.

"This is only the beginning," he whispered around her nipple before moving to the other tip and starting the seduction all over again. If she wished for a tryst, he would enter into it wholeheartedly, for a sin was a sin.

Wasn't it?

Pushing the thought to the back recesses of his mind, he concentrated on her. Suckling, soothing with his tongue, he worried that hardened bud, teasing her to the best of his ability. When she shook from his attentions, he continued with more of the same, for he wanted her close to that edge, begging him to finish her.

"Thomas…" Her fingers curled into his shirt, and she clutched at his arm with one hand.

"Hmm?" When he rolled those sensitive peaks, starting at the root and moving upward with varying degrees of pressure, she cried out with apparent joy and attempted to press her body closer to his.

"You don't play fair," she finally managed to pant in between nips and nibbles the side of his neck.

"I'm willing to say when it comes to carnal endeavors, nothing is quite fair. It's merely a matter of who can survive the longest before breaking." And he couldn't wait to see what she looked like when she went over that edge.

"Braggart. Now you sound like the rogue you apparently used to be." There was nothing proper about her as she shoved a hand between their bodies while he continued torturing her breasts. Seconds later, Genevieve cupped his burgeoning erection through the fabric of his breeches. A groan left his throat and she smiled; it didn't bode well for him. "Did you think you would leave this stream unscathed?"

"I don't know what I expected, to be honest." There was something about this woman that kept him on the edge of wonder and terror, as if he were holding his breath, waiting to see what she would do next.

"Poor man. You need far more stimulation in your life." She stroked him through his breeches. "I wonder if you'll taste sweet or salty." And the fool woman licked her lips as she met his gaze. "Do you dare me to find out?"

"Bloody hell." His guttural utterance sounded overly loud in the silence of their surroundings. Would she be the death of him? Well, he wouldn't leave her to make the first volley in this war. Quicky, he yanked her hand from his person, and nearly sagged with temporary relief. "I believe we are well past that line now."

"I did warn you I'm not entirely the lady society would like for me to be."

That was one of the reasons she was so fascinating. He didn't quite trust the grin that curved her kiss-swollen lips. With a half growl half curse, he put a hand to the small of her back, tugging her close once more. "In this moment, that is entirely fine, for I am not the gentleman my position demands."

They would have this one-off time together, and that would be that, and if they were fortunate, no one in the village would be the wiser.

"I like the sound of that." Her voice was a purr which had his shaft tightening ever more painfully.

"Then let us move onto other, more exquisite things." As

Thomas put her into a loose embrace, he knocked her feet from beneath her. When she tumbled to the soft, night-cooled grass, he followed her down onto the earth.

"There is nothing more seductive than a woman in this sort of undress with passion staining her cheeks." Though it was difficult to see in the moonlight.

Her eyes glinted with appreciation. "I'd be willing to remove the shift if you want." Clearly, she was no shrinking violet. She squirmed beneath him, and seconds later, her gloriously bared legs framed his body. "What now? Surely this isn't the extent of your expertise?"

"Hardly. When did you become such a minx?" A groan left his throat, for he couldn't delay touching her any longer. Thomas kneeled between her bent knees.

"I've always been a bit wild since my Come Out year."

He snorted. "If I were a betting man, I'd wager it was since you turned sixteen." As he spoke, Thomas encouraged the hem of her shift up her legs to her waist. Then he gently parted her thighs, spread her open to his gaze. "And also, if I were to bet, I'd say no one has ever done *this* to you."

"You would win, for outside of kissing and a few touches or caresses, no man has ever touched me as intimately as you are about to." The breathlessness in her voice made the moment even more poignant. "I, um, haven't been *that* daring, it seems."

"Then I'm honored." In this, he would be her first, her teacher, the man she would always compare the act against, and it was quite heady stuff. And if he didn't get on with it, he'd spend in his breeches. Leaning down, fairly laying on the grass, he buried his face between her thighs and then licked her slick flesh.

"Oh, oh dear…" Her hips bucked, which only put her more firmly in his hold.

He answered with action over words. It took little time to encourage her tiny pearl out of hiding, and with each probe and flick of his tongue, it swelled while Genevieve's breath grew erratic.

"I…" She fisted a hand into the long grass and with the other, shoved her fingers into his hair.

Thomas moved over her button, worried the nub, suckled at it, gave it tiny nibbles until she squirmed from his ministrations, alternately trying to shove him away and hold him closer.

"If you want to fly, you must climb that mountain," he whispered against her flesh then tried to soothe the bud with his tongue.

"Oh!" Genevieve panted. She thrashed her head from side to side. "I feel like drowning, yet falling all at once." When she moved a hand to the back of his head, holding him to where she apparently needed him to be, he glanced upward to meet her gaze, and she nodded. "I need more."

"No doubt you do." But he did as she bid, and what was more, she was sweet on his tongue like clean water or the nectar from clover flowers. Then he added fingers to his play, sliding them in and out of her quivering passage. "If it grows too much, cry mercy."

"And give you the satisfaction of winning?" She snorted as her hips undulated. "Hardly." Then her body stiffened. "Thomas!" With a surprised sort of scream, she shattered. Her body shook; her inner muscles contracted around his fingers, and the dear woman pointed her toes as she rode that wave. "Dear heavens." She collapsed onto the ground and stared at him. "Who would have ever thought a vicar could know how to do… *that?*"

"Ha!" He chuckled, for how could he not? "I did tell you I am a former rogue."

"What a shame you aren't any longer," she managed to whisper.

A wave of satisfaction rose in his chest. "Then let us say that I am a rogue until we are both sated, sweaty, and exhausted, hmm?" Perhaps that slide down the hill into sin wouldn't be as bad as he thought.

"That sounds all too lovely, but now it is my turn to torture you." Genevieve righted herself and before he could move, she pounced on him. The force of her attack tipped him onto his back. They sprawled on the grass in a tangle of limbs. "Tit for tat, wouldn't you say? Perhaps when you go over the edge, it will be much like visiting heaven, and then you can thank me." And there was another grin that tightened his chest.

"I admire your tenacity after you must have already survived a strong release."

"Do shut up, Mr. Alderman. Too much talking." And then she proceeded to kiss him with stark abandon and a wild determination that held him captive.

Damn, damn, damn!

The woman drank from him as if he held the last drop of water on Earth; she devoured him as if she had no decorum at all. It had no doubt fled the moment he put his fingers on her. When she dragged her lips down the strong column of his throat, he shivered then contented himself with once more bedeviling her nipples.

"Turn over." Two taps of a curled fist to his shoulder managed to make the words sink into his lust-clouded brain.

"What?"

"Flip over onto your back."

"Why?"

"You shall discover that all the quicker once you do as I say." When he did as she asked, she made a sound much like the purr of a cat. "Excellent. You are quite teachable. I appreciate that." Then, with mischief shining in her eyes, made luminous in the moonlight, Genevieve slid down his body. Watching him in the shifting shadows, she swiftly undid the buttons on his frontfalls. "Let's see what I have to work with, and with any luck, I shall be quite surprised." As his hardened length tumbled into her palm, she gave a pleased chuckle that went straight through his stones and caused his shaft to twitch. "A well-hung vicar. Now that *is* heaven sent."

Heat infiltrated his neck and cheeks, coursed through his chest. "Gammon. I'm adequate." And he couldn't help teasing her further as a way to ignore the touch of her fingers on his manhood. "It's enough for you to work with, hmm?"

"Very." When she ran the tip of her tongue along her lower lip, he shivered. "Let us see how much *you* can take before you'll break." Up and down, she drew her hand along his shaft with her curled fingers about his girth. "So thick. So hard." As she spoke, she shook her head and held his gaze. "Lovely."

"Perhaps you should leave off." Strain graveled his voice. With every stroke of her hand, each brush of her fingers, he shuddered and widened his legs in anticipation.

"That would be the proper thing to do, but where is the fun in that?" With a slow grin, Genevieve leaned over him and just as slowly, she licked the tip of his shaft.

"Gigi!" His hiss was swallowed by the sounds of the night.

"Hush. I have long wanted to do this to a man, and knowing I will to a man of your caliber is all the more impressive." Kneeling, she continued to work him over with her hand while taking his length into the warm cavern of her mouth.

As her lips closed around his member, he nearly lost his mind. "Damn." One of his hands fisted into the grass. "You are going to kill me, Genevieve."

"We'll find out together." She hummed around him, and when she moved her hand down to cup his stones, his body twitched. "So sensitive," she murmured around his shaft, and the vibrations sent him into the next level of pleasure.

"Leave off," he warned for the night would be over far too early due to her innocent enthusiasm.

"No." Then she proceeded to apply various degrees of depth and suction to his erection, alternately squeezing his stones and returning to twist her fingers around his shaft as she worked to separate him from reality.

"Please." At this rate, he wouldn't survive. A moan left his throat as she licked the underside of his member, and when she slipped a hand beneath him to squeeze one of his buttocks, stark need shuddered down his spine to lodge in his stones. "Dear God,

Genevieve…" There was naught to do except bury his fingers into her long, slightly damp hair and thrust upward into her mouth. "Damn, but that feels far too good," he said mostly to himself, and it had been a long time indeed since he'd last had a woman pleasure him in this way.

Making sounds of happiness, she continued to work him over, and he bucked his hips, caught in a cycle of bliss and need. Briefly, she pulled off his shaft and grinned, her eyes sparkling in the moonlight. "Give in. Spend for me. Let me taste your essence."

"I… I don't…"

"Then couple with me. Bed me. I will gladly give you my innocence in exchange for this experience with you." Again, she took him into her mouth, bobbing up and down on him, faster and faster.

"Oh, God!" Desperation propelled the soft cry, and in that, he knew a truth that he refused to back down on. By her own admission, she was still an innocent, and by rights he couldn't take that from her even if she was adamant that she gave it over. It was a gift that should be saved for the man who would eventually be her husband… and he wasn't that man. She wasn't the type of woman he could have by his side for the rest of his life. With his attention on his thoughts, he relaxed his hold on control.

He broke, shattered, was hurtled over the edge of sanity into bliss, and still, Genevieve continued to work over his shaft as he thrust more and more erratically. The stronger his length pulsed, the higher he flew into the heavens, and damn it all, if she didn't swallow every bit of what he gave her.

Finally, it was over, and though his breathing was still labored, Thomas sank into the grass with a pleasant lethargy weighting his limbs. He laid an arm over his eyes to temporarily block her from his sight.

What have I done?

He should have left her untouched. Instead, he'd violated her when he'd had no right and let her do the same to him. She was an untried miss, an innocent in such things. Had this ruined her? Not in the ways that mattered, but he should have put a stop to it before it had ever started.

And what sort of gentleman turned vicar did that? Even for the release?

"God forgive me," he whispered as he struggled into a seated position. When Genevieve stared at him with awe and further wickedness in her eyes, unease and need twisted down his spine. Hot guilt poured through his chest as he sprang to his feet, doing up the buttons of his frontfalls as he went. "This cannot happen again. Not any of it."

She pouted, and that gesture nearly became his downfall. "But, nothing happened, not truly." Once she'd gained her feet, she propped her hands on her hips, and he tried not to stare at her hardened nipples through the shift's fabric but failed. "I'm still an innocent, and that wasn't my intention this night."

There was only so much a man could withstand, and she was trouble. Sin and scandal, surely. "Perhaps, but in the eyes of society, I've compromised you."

"Or rather, I was the one who compromised you." With the shake of her head, she marched back to where she'd left her clothing. "So you won't finish me then?"

As if he could. For all her daring, she apparently didn't know how that portion of a man's anatomy worked. "I will not, and as I said, anything like this between us is folly. We *must not* come together again."

For long moments, she stared at him. Then she blew out a breath and snatched her petticoat from the grass. "You are a coward, Mr. Alderman."

"Be that as it may, you know it's true. I am a vicar, and you are governess to my nieces." He shoved a hand through his hair. "That is all there can ever be."

"Why?" With jerky movements, she drew the garment on and then secured the ties about her waist.

"Because you said you would only marry a titled, rich man."

"Are you saying you would marry me if I didn't want that?"

"No. I need a helpmeet beyond reproach."

"Ah, and I exude sin."

How to answer that? Finally, he shrugged. "Besides, I am not a rogue any longer. It will already be far too tempting having you beneath my roof." Bloody hell, he shouldn't have told her that, for she was far too crafty not to use that against him.

"There is nothing in the Bible that says a man of the cloth cannot give a servant a quick toss every now and again."

Such skewed views. He shook his head. "You are far more than a servant, and worth much more than a hurried tryst."

"It doesn't need to be rushed," she said with a slow grin that once more lit fires into his blood.

Yes, most certainly this woman would kill him, and it would be a very satisfying way to expire. Thomas shook his head. "You should go back to the vicarage. I need to beg God's forgiveness."

Her grin faded to a frown. "As if I'm evil or bad, something you regret touching." Her swallow was audible. "As if being with me will somehow send you to hell?" When he remained silent while confusion wrapped around him, she tamped on what sounded suspiciously like a sob. "Fine. Stay out here, but I hope when you're imploring the heavens, you find some real truths as well instead of hiding behind a book that is open to many and varied interpretations."

In obvious outrage, she gathered her belongings, shoved them into the willow basket, and then she marched away, apparently not caring that she was still scandalously clothed.

"I am headed to hell for certain." Yet he couldn't discount the new way of looking at things that had infiltrated his ponderings thanks to Genevieve. *What am I going to do?* Then he fell to his knees and bowed his head. "Heavenly Father…"

CHAPTER NINE

July 30, 1817

"The post is here, Mr. Alderman."

Thomas glanced up from contemplating the first lines of the sermon he had been writing and nodded at the housekeeper as she brought in a few envelopes to the study. "Thank you."

"Miss Hasting has taken the girls to a neighboring farm to visit with the children there, and while they are busy, I believe she has plans to visit with her family."

He nodded. "I appreciate the update, for I had wondered why the house was so quiet." And the very mention of Genevieve had awareness prickling over his skin. In fact, the reason why his sermon writing was going slowly was because he could think of nothing other than her and what they'd done together two days ago.

"You shouldn't bury yourself in your study so much, Vicar. There is more to living than writing sermons and worrying over your parishioners."

"So I am beginning to realize." He waved her off. "I do have work to attend all the same, but I promise to surface for tea."

"Ring if you should need anything." Then she left him to his thoughts.

Which were more confusing than ever. Though he'd asked God to forgive him the trespass with his nieces' governess, that hadn't evicted her from his mind. All he could see was her gorgeous legs on display, remembered the warmth and feel of her breasts against his palms and fingertips, how her lips had cradled his, how she'd tasted when he'd pleasured her with his mouth as if he'd been depraved.

What the hell is wrong with me?

With nothing else to do, Thomas broke the seal on the first letter, which was from Vicar Addington, the man who held the living before him. He'd stayed on for a month in order to teach Thomas how the church worked in the small area, he'd introduced him to some of the more prominent residents—including Genevieve's parents—and he'd given more than a few lectures on how to maintain order within his flock. Afterward, he had moved to a comfortable cottage somewhere in Surrey to live out his retirement.

Now he'd written to Thomas.

Knots of worry pulled in his gut as he unfolded the missive, and they continued to tighten as he read through the letter.

...there is gossip in the air stating your marital status is becoming disruptive and proving a distraction. Perhaps it's time for you to take a bride. In doing so you will become a better leader of the church. It's best to nip this current problem in the bud. Women should not attend the church merely to lust after a handsome vicar...

Was the man truly holding his looks against him? He couldn't help that he was more attractive than the average man. Did the former vicar believe that only ugly men should hold the position? With a huff of annoyance, Thomas continued to read the letter.

...if this matter is not attended to with the utmost urgency, I'm afraid I shall make certain you are removed from the living. I

shall have someone else installed there who can uphold the position and maintain the image the lost sheep need...

Why was it that something bad always canceled out the good? Fate or God's plan? It was too difficult to know, especially from a lowly human standpoint.

...either find yourself engaged within the next month, Thomas, or expect a visit from someone much higher up in the Church than I am. We simply cannot have you creating a sensation when you are supposed to be leading a congregation away from sin...

Bah. There were simply no good paths to trod at the moment.

Once more, Mrs. Traverse came to the open door of his study. "There is a Lord Grantford here to see you, Mr. Alderman."

"What?" In some agitation, he folded the letter and stuffed it back into the envelope. "Alex is here? In Bedfordshire?" He hadn't seen the viscount in what seemed like an age. Certainly not since Thomas had left London.

"So it would seem. I have put him into the parlor," the housekeeper said with amusement threading through her voice.

"Ah, show him in here, and then bring tea. It's much less formal here, and he is my best friend, after all." Apprehension circled through his gut as he slowly rose to his feet. Why the devil was he here?

"Of course, Mr. Alderman."

Seconds later following the housekeeper's departure, the viscount came into the study looking for all the world as if he were ready to drive a curricle along Rotten Row. A jacket of bottle-green superfine highlighted his broad chest and shoulders, and paired with a golden satin waistcoat and tan-colored breeches along with shiny Hessian-style boots, he was every inch a peer of the *beau monde*.

"Alex! It's been far too long." Thomas came around his desk with a hand extended. "What brings you by my tiny slice of the world?"

"I thought to check in on you since correspondence hasn't been forthcoming."

The viscount shook the offered hand, then they both moved to the side of the room and dropped onto a low sofa of soft leather he'd gained second hand. It was comfortable enough to sleep on, which he'd discovered the past couple of nights, for being across a narrow corridor from where Genevieve slept was too great a temptation.

"So, you sought me out." Thomas frowned, for that sounded far too suspicious. "Or did someone send you?"

"I'm here of my own volition." Grantford removed his top hat and tossed it to the low table in front of the sofa. "I have truly missed prowling about Town with you." His golden hair glimmered in the sunlight streaming in through a window. It highlighted his nearly perfect teeth and the set of his angular jaw.

The summer breeze coming into the room was fragrant with flowers. "Well, if it's any consolation, my life is considerably duller now that I'm a vicar."

"I'll wager it is," the viscount said with a chuckle.

When the housekeeper returned with a tea tray, which she set on the table, Thomas nodded his thanks and then immediately poured out two cups, one he handed to his friend.

"Why did you do it, Thomas? Why the devil would you ever want to become a vicar and give up the life you used to have?" There was nothing but honesty in his friend's face and voice.

"I received a call from God to minister to his flock."

Grantford snorted. "Or was it because you'd landed in far too many scandals and needed somewhere to hide?"

"At the time, my parents were annoyed with the sensations I'd caused." Thomas's lips twitched from amusement. "However, I am dead serious about this position. I truly enjoy being a vicar and watching over my congregation. Well, that is to say, most days."

One of the viscount's eyebrows rose in question. "Meaning?"

Knowing he could trust his friend with his life—and they had more than enough secrets on each other to provoke discretion—Thomas blew out a breath. "There are the usual temptations, of course. Temptations I am unable to act upon."

After taking a deep drink of tea, the viscount nodded. "I can understand that. You were quite a favorite of the ladies in London. A man like you couldn't merely leave that life behind without some sort of withdrawal symptoms."

"Perhaps not, and eventually willpower crumbles."

"Oh? Have you met someone?" Surprise threaded through Alex's tone.

"I don't know." Fearful of being overheard, Thomas left the sofa, crossed the room, and softly closed the door. As he returned to his seat, he glanced at the open window to be sure no one lurked outside. Still, he lowered his voice. "It all began when I hired a governess for my nieces."

"Ah." A slow grin skated across the viscount's face. "I thought you had a different look about you, as if you are… happy, like the man I used to know when we'd knocked about Town together in the old days."

Heat went up the back of Thomas's neck. "I don't know if I'm happy. In fact, I have done something highly improper." In a low tone and succinct words, he told Alex what had transpired between him and Genevieve a couple of nights ago. "Though it wasn't full on intercourse, and I never penetrated her body with my shaft, she has been ruined all the same." He shook his head then drained his teacup. "It was improper on more than a few levels."

A chuckle left the viscount's throat. His eyes twinkled with mischief. "But do you feel alive?"

"I do, in more ways than I expected." It was an admission he would die to protect.

Grantford shrugged. "Then where is the harm? You entered

into a bit of slap and tickle with a willing," he threw a glance at Thomas, "I assume she was willing?"

"Oh, yes. Very much so, and she was the one who instigated the whole thing."

"Then I don't see why you should be wracked by guilt."

"Of course you don't." As a bit of annoyance coursed through his veins, Thomas set his teacup onto the table. "Miss Hasting is my nieces' governess. I'm a man of God. There should be standards, propriety—"

"Gammon." His friend leaned back and rested an ankle on a knee. "Miss Hasting is a woman and you're a man." With a wink, he took another gulp of tea. "You never took a vow of chastity when you became a vicar. If you are discreet, where is the harm?"

He snorted. "I am not that man any longer, though. In fact, I am trying to be a better man." And he was failing miserably at it.

"I understand that." When the viscount glanced at the window, he frowned. "Where is Miss Hasting at the moment?"

"She apparently escorted the girls to a neighboring farmer so they could play with other children then she had planned to visit with her own parents." He blew out a breath. "We haven't spoken candidly or at length since that night. I... I think she's in a snit with me."

"Can you blame her?" Grantford chuckled again. "You did the worst thing imaginable. Not finishing her off and then spouting off religious nonsense which may or may not have indicated she was somehow less than savory?" A low whistle escaped him. "You are fortunate a snit is all you've gotten from her."

"But not coupling her was the lesser of the two evils." He couldn't help it if Genevieve had wished for more. "She's an innocent, man. I didn't want to corrupt her."

"It sounds as if she's the one leading *you* on a merry chase. You should have done the deed." Mischief remained high as he looked at Thomas "Do you still wish to?"

For the space of a few heartbeats, he remained silent. Then he finally nodded. "God, yes. I cannot remove her from my thoughts."

"Then perhaps after you bed her, all of that will go away. The urges will leave your system and you can resume your dull, placid life."

"Yet she is... irresistible." It was a hopeless cause, really. Rubbing a hand along the side of his face, he frowned. "There is just something about her..." It was an impossible match between them, at best. Truly, they had no future together beyond perhaps heat.

"You are heading into dangerous territory, my friend." An intense expression came over Grantford's face. "Do you want to marry her? If you do, then you can bed her without the guilt."

There was that, and it was the easiest solution. Yet he shrugged. "I am not in love with her, and neither does she have those feelings for me."

"That doesn't matter, and you know it. We come from a world where many unions are based in mutual regard and respect instead of love."

"Right, but it matters to me. I want to love the woman I would speak vows to." Everything was a mess, and it needed to stop with him. Perhaps spending more time in prayer would help... or telling Genevieve her governess services weren't wanted any longer. Which would damage his relationship with his nieces. Then he cleared his throat. "Even if I did wish to marry her, she doesn't want a poor man. Genevieve hopes to marry well to be a lady of leisure, and I need a proper woman who can help lead my flock."

One of the viscount's eyebrows rose. "You use her Christian name?"

Another wave of heat went up the back of his neck. "After what we've already shared, that is hardly scandalous."

"True." He gazed at Thomas with speculation in his eyes. "Continue."

Thomas nodded. "While she is a delight and she challenges me at every turn as well as inflames my desire, she isn't who I need by my side." Her behavior, her forward-thinking attitude, her previous scandals would all but destroy his living and perhaps his future.

"Then enjoy her now in whatever capacity you see fit. Afterward, settle down with a woman more suited to your lifestyle and calling. There is no harm in getting your jollies off before you marry elsewhere."

The words had need shivering down his shift, forcing him to shift in his seat. Having a fling with Gigi without remorse yet not destroying his future. Could it even be done? "Perhaps. But it's against the Bible's teaching." There was no denying that, and didn't that book contain the rules he should live by?

And if that were true, then there was no recourse except to begin courting someone that wasn't her, which would eventually lead to removing Genevieve from her position. The thought of that sent sour bile up the back of his throat.

Grantford cleared his throat, recalling Thomas's attention. "Can you look me in the eye and honestly tell me that you believe no one in the Bible ever had sexual relations beyond or outside the bounds of marriage?"

"Well, I…"

"Or that men married and then still took mistresses?" the viscount continued as if Thomas hadn't spoken.

"Of course it's possible, but…"

"Such things have been the same throughout the centuries since time began." He grinned. "God will *not* strike you down for the mere fact that being with this woman brings you pleasure, or heaven forbid, happiness. Everyone knows you deserve at least that after the past couple of years you've endured."

"Are grief, frustration, and compassion grounds to bed the governess, though?" When he met his friend's gaze, they both chuckled. "I suppose I've done the same for less." He rubbed his eyes. "I have been put on notice by the old vicar. He says if I don't marry someone suitable, he will petition the powers-that-be and have me removed from this post." Did it annoy him that someone else was poking around in his private affairs? Of course, but what could he do?

"Ah, then you are well and truly cocked." His friend straightened and put both feet flat on the floor. "I'm afraid you'll have to make a decision."

"Where I'll come out the loser all the way 'round." Never did he think he'd be facing such things when he'd taken this living. "I always knew I'd marry, just didn't assume it would be so soon or because of my looks."

"And the fact you cannot keep your hands off the governess," Grantford was quick to add with a cheeky grin.

"There is that." He couldn't help but grin. "Perhaps you might enjoy a glass of brandy to complement your tea? I certainly do."

"Here, here," Grantford said as he lifted his teacup in salute. "In the meantime, you can tell me about the marriage options within your flock, and if any compare with the scandalous Miss Hasting."

Thomas remained silent on that, for there simply was no one like her. If there were, he hadn't met them yet.

CHAPTER TEN

ONCE GRANTFORD LEFT—AFTER promising to spend a week in the area—Thomas still couldn't concentrate on his sermon writing. The girls hadn't returned, neither had Genevieve, and it was too early for dinner, so he took himself off for a walk, hoping the exercise would calm the restlessness of his body and quell the heat in his blood.

He didn't know how long or how far he'd walked, but his mind hadn't cleared, nor had he succeeded in removing the governess from his thoughts. And damn, it was deuced hot.

A tiny miracle occurred when the sun ducked behind a large cluster of fat, fluffy clouds, but he wasn't so fortunate about his thoughts. As if he'd conjured her from thin air, Gigi appeared on the road ahead, obviously coming from the direction of her father's property.

He tipped his face to the sky. *Why are you testing me, God?* Was he to go through a set of trials like Job? Or perhaps he would be turned into a pillar of salt like Lot's wife for disobedience. Neither were favorable choices.

It wasn't until she came much closer that he spied a trace of moisture on her face and lingering in her eyes beneath her bonnet. When she finally glanced at him, she offered him a wobbly smile. "Hullo, Thomas." Dust and dirt had marred the hem of the pale blue walking dress as well as the toes of the half boots she wore. "Uh, have the girls been escorted home yet?"

"They hadn't been when I set out." He came a few steps closer and peered more fully into her face. "Are you well?" Worry knotted in his gut. Was she still out of sorts about what occurred—or not—between them the other night? It seemed he was largely still a coward, for he couldn't bring himself to ask. "Has something happened with your parents?"

"Everything is fine." When she attempted to move past him, he stepped into her path.

"You are either not skilled in lying or you are too upset to try." Not able to remain parted from her, he gently rested a gloved hand on her shoulder. "What has you at sixes and sevens? I want to help if I can." Perhaps focusing on her problems would make him forget about the unrelenting lust that flowed through his body with all the heat of lava.

"I don't know if anyone can help right now." She sounded so forlorn that his chest tightened, and his heart squeezed.

"Tell me what happened." Then he took her hand and threaded it through his crooked elbow as he set them into motion on the empty road. "Don't think of me as your vicar; I am merely a friend." A friend who compromised the hell out of her and they hadn't talked about that since the night.

Gigi's hand trembled on his sleeve. "Once the girls were safely at their friends' farm, I walked over for a visit with my parents, since seeing them on Sundays just doesn't feel like enough."

"That's understandable." For the most part, he remained silent, for he didn't wish to break her concentration.

"I arrived in time for tea; Mama and Papa had just sat down. My younger sisters were also there. Nora was apparently out on an errand." When she held her lush bottom lip briefly between her teeth, his world nearly spun, for the gesture only made him want to kiss her. "It would have been a lovely time except…"

"Yes?"

Her swallow was audible, and her fingers tightened on his arm. "My father's condition has rapidly declined. Today, he barely recognized me." The waver in her voice had him wanting to throw himself on his knees to beg her forgiveness and to pledge his life to her, so he could protect her, have the right to do that and so many other things. "Mama said it wasn't one of his better days. She reassured me that he wasn't always like that."

The poor thing. "What did you do?" He couldn't imagine trying to interact with a family member who barely knew him.

"What could I do? I kept telling him who I was, and that he was my father." She shook her head and brushed at the tears on her cheeks with her free hand. "It was so sad, Thomas! I don't know what I'll do once he fades completely from this world."

"Such is the human experience, I'm afraid. We all have an expiration date, which is why it's so important that we love and cherish those around us while we can." Damn, if that couldn't fit into his situation as well.

"And my poor mother. She grows weaker with every passing week. I think having Nora at home as well as Papa's health is wearing on her." For long moments, she remained silent. "My sister Emmaline is thinking of conducting painting lessons for coin. She's offered to teach the girls one day a week if I walk them over."

"That sounds reasonable. I can no doubt find the funding for that." And it would keep Genevieve with him all the longer.

"It's appreciated. Even though my older sisters continue to send money home when they're able, I'm afraid it isn't enough, for at times, Mama cannot apply it to the taxes."

"Where is it going?"

She snorted, no doubt near a breaking point. "Food, drink, paying the servants what she can." A half-stifled sob escaped her throat. "There is always something to pay, and I'm so afraid for them." When she stepped a bit closer to his side, as if she were seeking comfort, he patted her hand. It simply wouldn't do to slip an arm about her in public where anyone could come upon them on the road. "I spied a letter saying the tax assessor would visit the manor soon to discuss future plans."

"Oh, Gigi, I'm so sorry." If their manor were lost, where would they go? "Perhaps you can all go up to London and live with... Amelia, is it? And her viscount?"

"I suppose." Tears threatened in her voice. "It's all just so much. I cannot let myself think on it; it will tear me apart." She sniffled, tugged on his arm, and drew him to a halt. As she stared up at him and their gazes connected, he was in danger of falling into the blue pools of her eyes and drowning. "I don't want to go back to the vicarage just yet."

"Why?" Had he suddenly lost the ability to converse like an intelligent man in her presence?

She shrugged. "It's too... proper, respectable." When she smiled, it was a watery affair. "It might sound silly to you, but I need to do something crazy to distract me from reality." As she tried to pull away, he kept hold of her hand. "I don't care if you think it's wrong; it's what I'm feeling. I'm not as good or as strong as you, I guess."

In many ways, Genevieve was like a lost lamb. Protection welled for her. "I am not perfect, and neither am I on a pedestal." It was important that she understand that. "I constantly fall short of being honorable or holy."

After she blew out a breath, she nodded. "Perhaps, but there is nothing that says you must be either. Just because you're a vicar doesn't mean you should keep yourself locked away from everything that might bring joy or happiness or pleasure."

Not this again. He was far too exhausted and ruffled in spirit to have such an argument. "I can only do what I can. If that makes me weak in the spine, so be it." Perhaps that was the only way she would lose interest in him.

"Ha. Now who is the one dissembling?" When she met his gaze once more, her moisture-spiked lashes captured his imagination. The moisture magnified her eyes and made them luminous. "Why does everyone associated with the Church believe they must be dull in order for them to live a good and wholesome life? Do you really think God wishes to deny his followers excitement or intimate connection?"

"Well, I—"

Apparently, she was only starting her discourse. "For that matter, do you truly believe God wants you to live stuck between the pages of a Bible as if you were a pressed flower, that your *only* purpose in life is to deliver sermons and bring the lost to Him? That you don't deserve notice or to be admired?"

"I hadn't given that much thought." None of it was making him think of her as only one of his parishioners, so he forced a swallow into his suddenly dry throat. "What do *you* believe?" Perhaps that would help him understand her better.

"I believe that a deity who spent so much time in making a world such as this, in developing so many different kinds of animals and people and environments wouldn't want any of his creations to suffer or hold themselves aloof. He would want you to enjoy everything He has given you."

"That's true enough, but sin—"

"No. It's a tactic the Church uses for control, to keep people in line and giving tithes, which line leaders' pockets." She shook her head so hard, a lock of hair tumbled from beneath her bonnet. "I think if you found yourself before God at the end of your life, He would ask you why you didn't love and enjoy things and people. Why you taught others that they could only worship Him in a church and not out in nature where there is His glory everywhere one looks."

"Yes, but—"

She wasn't having his interruptions. "God would be puzzled by the fact the Church decrees the only purpose for love making is reproduction and not enjoyment." When she narrowed her eyes, they shot blue lightning. "Why the devil would God give humans the capacity to feel ecstasy, to soar in bliss with another person—which is the closest we can probably ever be to experiencing that perfect love God has for his Church—if we weren't supposed to chase that high?"

"Oh, Gigi." In many ways, her questions were like the ones he'd uttered in seminary school, where some of his teachers couldn't find decent answers. Had he forgotten the early vim and vigor he had during those early days when he could still think for himself? "I adore the fact that you encourage me to dig deeper."

"Well… good, because you are better than the masses." She stalked away from him as her temper flared, and damn his eyes, she was magnificent. "Further, I don't understand why anyone would say everything good and lovely was bad or against the Church's teachings if not to control the populace. Have those stodgy old men in charge never known what it is to love, to give themselves to someone or something, to take in the beauty, the glory, the all-consuming feelings that make us remember we are indeed alive? Wouldn't that encourage them to think more fondly of God, or to see him as loving instead of vengeful?"

He unexpectedly lost a piece of his heart to her in that moment, and he desperately wished to rekindle his own fire. "All good points. I appreciate your perspective," he said as he caught up to her.

"Yet you won't change." Her sigh sounded all too defeated. "For all your talk of just that, you *are* a prisoner to the Church, of their dictates, some man's opinions. That's a pity." She glanced at him with her eyes the color of deep blue sapphires in the filtered sunlight. "Go on with your walk. I'll go alone… somewhere."

Puzzlement immediately set in, for his mind still reeled from her impassioned speech. "Why?"

"I am still out of sorts with you and quite disillusioned." Then her chin quivered, a sure sign she was close to a breaking point. "Perhaps I am also a tad disappointed, and I don't like having all these feelings." She took a few steps away from him. "I'm going into the village. There is a young man there who will give me what I need without the lectures or the sermon."

Over my dead and quite cold body. "No."

"What?" As her lips turned down in a frown, she shook her

head. "The girls don't need me at present—"

"Exactly," he interrupted as one final decision swept over him. "You are coming with me."

She scoffed. "Why should I? After all, aren't I the human equivalent of Sodom and Gomorrah? Isn't that what you tried to impart the other night? A weight about your ankle that will drown you in sin?"

"I am quite sorry I said those things. Obviously, they aren't true." To a point. Unless that wasn't what he truly thought, and his mind was steeped in confusion. Heat crept up his neck. "I didn't mean that."

"Then you shouldn't have said it."

"Oh, I am well aware of that, and have berated myself ever since." He tugged at the knot of his cravat. "You challenge me in every conceivable way." It needed to be said again.

Genevieve shrugged, but her expression softened a bit. "I suppose you don't like that either."

In this moment, he refused to debate with himself on what was right or what was wrong. He only knew that he wanted her, that his world wouldn't be complete until he had joined with her body, taught her everything he knew, and they were left sated and exhausted. Only then could she truly be out of his blood. "On the contrary." Beyond caring about propriety or proper behavior, Thomas hauled her into his arms, brought his mouth crashing down on hers, and he proceeded to kiss her thoroughly. Afterward, when he released her, she stumbled, and he grinned. "Do you wish to come with me or not? There will be no lectures."

Her eyes had rounded and darkened with the same desire coursing through his veins. "That depends."

"On?" Need caused his pulse to pound and his shaft to follow suit.

"What *my* incentive is in such an action."

Little minx. He put his lips to her ear and then whispered, "Bliss and filthy, unrepentant sin, Miss Hasting." When she gasped, he kissed her again, because he could. "I intend to send you flying until you cry mercy. I shall worry over the state of my soul and yours later, damn the consequences."

Perhaps she wasn't the only one who could make impassioned speeches.

"I'm quite proud of you, Mr. Alderman, so I accept your premise." She held out her hand and when he grasped it, she grinned. "I look forward to seeing how you make your case for scandal."

There were worse ways to spend a late July afternoon, and Thomas couldn't wait to start.

CHAPTER ELEVEN

*S*URELY, *THIS IS* madness, *folly certainly.*

Gigi's heartbeat tripped through her veins as Thomas practically ran with her along the road, and then when they left the hard-packed earth to flee through the rolling fields of tall grasses, flutters of anticipation bedeviled her.

Merciful heavens. He had been commanding and scandalous all in one when he'd kissed her and then whispered what he intended to do to her—with her—and it had surprised her, for she hadn't thought it possible he could be that sort of man. Though he'd apparently been a rogue in his past, it delighted her that he'd chosen to return to that man now, and she couldn't help but trembling in anticipation.

"Where are we going?"

"There is a barn not far from here. I'm confident it's used for little more than storing dry straw and perhaps other implements of farming." A wicked, intense light danced in his eyes when he spared her a glance. "Besides, the sheep are grazing, so the farmer shouldn't be along until near sunset."

"A barn?"

"Yes. Do you take exception with that?"

"Absolutely not." She tightened her hold on his hand. Some of her fondest memories had occurred in barns, from falling in love with horses and spending time with them—before her father had been forced to sell them—to more recently meeting handsome groomsmen and men from the village in barns or mews for a few moments alone for kissing or fondling.

"Good."

Then the barn came into view, and she marveled that she hadn't paid the structure much mind. Fairly weathered, sunlight showed through some of the cracks between the board, but there was a large hayloft where straw peeked through the open side. In the far distance, white dots of sheep were evident, and she'd never noticed.

Possibly because there was always something preying on her mind when she came through this stretch of road. Especially now.

"Come, Miss Hasting. It is time for us both to revisit scandal." The second they entered the barn, he tugged her into his arms. The attraction present between them caught fire and sucked them into its vortex as he kissed her thoroughly and quite relentlessly... and she couldn't have enough of him. His lips were firm but yielding and insistent, and she gave him back everything he offered. Perhaps took even more, for she had craved this moment with him since setting eyes on him. All too soon tongues were entwined, and hands were exploring until she had his cravat loosened and the ribbons of her bonnet had been untied. The headgear fell to the barn floor, forgotten.

"Damn, Genevieve, you are quite the addiction," he whispered, and the shocked desire in his eyes was all the encouragement she needed. He pitched his top hat to the ground where it bounced and rolled a few feet away. "I fear what it will do to us both."

"I know the feeling, but as you said, this afternoon is not for worrying." Gigi wrenched out of his arms. The yearning to feel his touch, his possession, was too strong to ignore. "Let's move into a more private area." She took his hand and led him toward a ladder.

As soon as they went further into the building, the pungent scent of farm animals, straw, and leather filled her nose. No beasts were in residence, and the few stalls had already been mucked out—or never used—another clue the tenant wouldn't return until nightfall. Feeling reckless and uninhibited, as Gigi climbed a wooden ladder to the hayloft above, she made certain her hip movements were exaggerated, and hoped he looked his fill. "Never let anyone doubt you are every bit a virile man," she said as they gained the loft.

"I'll admit, there have been times during this living that have been more frustrating than others. It is difficult to separate me the vicar and me the man."

"Perhaps you don't need to, for they are one and the same. Trust yourself." So easily Gigi returned to his arms. She kissed him with the verve and enthusiasm she had done for everything in her life, but doing so with him felt right, as if she'd waited for just this moment.

"Concentrate of the now, you mean."

"Yes. Truly, it is how I have survived unpleasant changes in recent years," she whispered against his lips while reaching for his cravat. "And even then, I don't think I'm doing a good job of seeing them through with grace."

"Grace is a skill one must practice."

"As is giving pleasure…"

Various bits of clothing fell to the fragrant, clean straw: his jacket, her dress and the ribbon about her waist, their gloves, his waistcoat, cuffs, collar, and cravat. Then he pulled his shirt from his body the same time Gigi removed her petticoat and stepped out of it.

"You are the most erotic sight," he breathed as he quickly worked the laces of her stays.

She cut his words off with a fierce kiss. "No talking. At least not right now." When she slowly removed the shift from her person and let it drop to the hay, Thomas gaped at her. "Well?" As outspoken as she was, Gigi had never been naked in front of a man before, and nerves beset her. "Do I pass or at the very least come up to the mark of the ladies you must have bedded in London?" Surely, he didn't consider her a country bumpkin.

"You have no idea how beautiful you are, Genevieve." Reverence threaded through his voice as he tugged off his boots. They fell to the boards of the loft with two resounding thuds. "I'm honored you chose me." Then he kneeled on the straw, looked expectantly at her until she joined him. Seconds later, he helped her remove her stockings, garters, and slippers.

"Honestly, there is no one better." When she reached for him, he reared backward and struggled out of his shirt. "There has been heat between us from the first."

"Agreed." A wicked grin curved his sensuous lips as she leaned back onto her elbows to let him look his fill. "Siren."

"Leading men to their death or a country vicar to hell?"

"Forgiveness is easier to come by, so I'm blindly following in this moment." With a knee between her legs, he spread open her thighs and then settled himself in the cradle of her hips.

This is truly going to happen!

There was nothing else to say, not that she could, for he'd claimed her lips again with the same passion he had each time they'd ever kissed. Why had she not known how heavenly kissing could be? Why had her sisters not told her that having a man's lips upon her own would both make her want to sing and to faint at the same time? Thomas pulled away long enough to strip out of his breeches, but when he came back and his naked body pressed into hers with his hardened length hot and twitching at her hip, she wanted to cry out with joy and relief.

He must think I'm a silly goose or a ninny of an innocent.

"I can almost hear you think," he whispered against her lips.

"Oh? It's not seconds thoughts, just fears that I'm not as sophisticated as the women you have known before."

"There are many different sorts of women. You are wonderful in your own way, and I adore that unique gift."

"Ah." The words were quite romantic. She lifted her chin

when he dragged his lips down the side of her neck. At her collarbones, he licked the hollow between them, and when she tried to caress him, he tsked his tongue. Catching her wrists in his hands, he shoved her arms above her head.

"Leave them there while I explore every curve you possess." The same vestiges of forcefulness entered his voice like she'd detected before they'd reached the barn, and it sent shivers down her spine.

"And if I don't?" What else would he do if provoked? Suddenly, there was a new element to their play, and it had barely started.

"Then I'll be forced to tie you to one of those posts... and I rather think that's too extreme for your first time." The wicked gleam in his eyes left her breathless, but his hands on her breasts made her want to cry out in delight.

"I... Oh..." Even though she suspected some of what would happen ahead of intercourse, Gigi was unprepared to be immediately swamped with intense sensations. She curled her fingers into the fragrant straw she lay on, for every pass of his fingers, each time he rubbed them over her hard, sensitive nipples caused a cascade of pleasure down her spine and through her lower belly. But when he took one of those stiff peaks into the warm cavern of his mouth, she moaned and her back arched. "That is amazing."

"It's quite the point of this exercise." He chuckled into her skin. "Why else would people engage in sexual congress?"

"I... don't know." Her ability to think of words, let alone utter them, was rapidly slipping away the longer he played with her nipples.

Stroking. Teasing. Sucking. Biting. Soothing with his tongue until she moaned and writhed beneath him, asking him to stop but urging him to continue. What he did to her didn't compare to the experimental and rushed fumblings she'd shared with various men in an effort to touch them and have them do the same to her. This was different... adult... no going back.

"Thomas, I…" What? Words flew right out of her head, for she was nearly drowning in what he was doing to her. "This is so much better than when I pleasure myself."

"What?" He stopped his ministrations to stare at her. Shock and desire clouded his eyes. "You touch yourself?"

"Yes. A few times a month in my bed at night when I feel restless and cannot explain it." She swallowed, hoping it didn't mean she was bound for hell over that. "I learned from some of the maids over the years and watching trysts between the servants." Then she shrugged. "Also, my married friends talk."

"Every facet to you I uncover sparkles more brilliantly than the last. In short, you are fascinating." The wicked man began his heady torture all over again. She shook from his attentions; her body was so hot she feared she would burst into flame, but it was the loveliest adventure she'd ever embarked upon.

"Let me touch you," she managed to gasp while commanding her eyes to open. If she didn't, she would soon be swept away and let him do all the delicious things to her like a boring woman.

Which she was not.

"Later." He batted her hands away from his shaft. "I'll explode soon, and your touch will only send me there faster, for it has been years since I've lain with a woman."

Was that a compliment? She didn't know and hesitated to ask for it would interrupt the lovely tension and pressure building inside her body. "You've denied yourself enough as a vicar. Surely, it's time to play."

"Gigi, no, I mean it."

"I never am one to follow a man's dictates, though." Unable to keep her hands to herself, she curled one about his nape, guided him to a nipple while she caressed her free hand up and down his arm. Oh, such a solid form! "It is a crime you hide beneath somber clothing." Suddenly, she wished to learn everything about him beyond how he kept himself fit.

A growl escaped him, and the sound was so foreign to the person he was she stared. "I thought I told you not to move your hands."

"I couldn't help it." She gasped for air. His touch, the heat of him, the rasp of his course chest hair on her sensitive nipples, the sound of his voice threatened to drown her. "Let me be a part of my own ruin."

For that was exactly what faced her, and gladly would she give up her innocence without a second thought. Perhaps she might become with child, perhaps not, but she would worry over that possibility when and if it materialized. Such an occurrence would further throw her family into scandal, but she didn't care.

She wanted this. Needed this.

Needed *him* in this moment. Something about him called to something in her, and she'd never had that connection with anyone before. Why shouldn't she explore it?

"I have never met anyone like you." He kissed her mouth. "You might become a bad influence in my life, but I cannot help but ignore the warning in my head. I want you, must possess you."

The words sent a host of shivers along her spine. How thrilling this whole act was. "Be careful, Vicar, for I might find I like this sort of scandal far too much to let you go."

"We shall see." Thomas glided a hand slowly down her body, between her breasts, along her torso, over her abdomen. Gooseflesh trailed after him, and when he buried his fingers into her curls, she gasped in anticipation. "I won't apologize for any of it."

"I'm not asking you to. In this moment, you are not a vicar and I am not a governess." She sucked in a breath when he eased those digits along that most private part of her that no man had ever touched. "We are merely two people who desperately need an outlet and a break from a life that has suddenly become overwhelming." A surprised yelp was yanked from her throat, for he'd slid a finger along her folds until he uncovered that tiny bud at her center that made her world spark and spin.

"Then let me make you fly again. It was quite erotic the last time." The earl took possession of her lips while he continued to bedevil that little button.

"Oh, oh!" The varying degrees of friction drove her mad, and he was quite skilled. Too bad his knowledge was wasted on his insistence on being in the Church. Her hips bucked off the straw, which caused his engorged length to bump along her inner thigh. Lord, but she couldn't wait to feel him inside her body. Gigi dug her fingernails into his shoulder, she licked and nipped and kissed any part of him she could reach. A moan echoed and she pulled slightly away, breaking their kisses, but he continued with his dizzying torment. Wave upon wave of pleasure burst through her consciousness, and she rode them out while her core shuddered, and her belly fluttered.

And the invisible thread that connected them tightened a bit more.

"What are you doing to me? I don't feel myself any longer." Vaguely aware she'd spoken the words aloud, she moved her hips in hopes he would send her flying again. "That was…" She had no words. "I very much want to experience that again." If this was scandalous in the eyes of the matrons of society, they were utterly and completely wrong, and she felt sorry for them.

Perhaps they needed more of this in their lives.

"I don't believe I said I was done with you," Thomas whispered against the shell of her ear. He suckled one of her breasts and eased off. "Did you truly think that I wouldn't bedevil a woman like you as many times that I could while I have access to your body?" Those talented fingers slid over her flesh that had dampened from his attentions. Then he penetrated her body with two of those digits, stroking, pumping, stretching. When she whimpered with need—surely something would relieve the terrible pressure circling through her insides—he pressed his thumb to her throbbing button. The two sensations were unlike anything she'd ever known before, and nothing like she could have ever done to herself.

She would be lost all too soon.

"Thomas, I need more." If that was too bold, she didn't care. It was her ruination, and she would have it in a spectacular way.

"Then that is what you shall have."

The moment he closed his mouth onto a pebbled nipple, she moaned and arched her back while he kneaded her other breast. The scent of straw, combined with the lighter smell of his cologne or shaving soap that imparted notes of pine and freshly fallen snow, enhanced everything he did to her somehow. When he nuzzled the crook of her shoulder, nipped and nibbled a path between her breasts, over them, explored her navel while he continued to pleasure her with his fingers, she tried not to break apart from the intense stimulation.

"This is..." Gigi gasped for breath as she squirmed from his play. "This is wonderful." *Oh, dear heavens!* The wicked man dipped his head between her splayed thighs and drew his tongue along her folds. "Thomas!" It merely made her remember their time together a couple of days ago, and she further sank into the swirling vortex of sensations. As he chuckled against her skin, he encouraged that tiny bud at her center out of hiding and then set to work worrying it with his lips, alternately sucking it into his mouth and soothing it with swipes of his tongue. "I cannot last..." But she held his head tightly against her flesh, showing him exactly where she needed him. In the next second she attempted to shove him away, for the feelings were so intense she might expire, but he was stubborn.

And he didn't stop his erotic torment.

"Oh!" A keening cry left Gigi's throat the second he increased the friction against that nubbin. She squirmed, thrashed her head into the straw. "Thomas!" She curled the fingers of one hand into his hair as if he alone would keep her anchored to this world.

"I'd say that was quite satisfactory for you, hmm?" Pure masculine smugness sounded in his voice as he came back up her body.

"Careful, Mr. Alderman. I could become all too accustomed to this, and it is quite a lovely way to spend a summer afternoon."

Nothing else mattered except chasing the next high.

"Ha." Thomas cut off her words with a kiss that was so poignant it knocked all thoughts from her mind. "I can delay claiming you no longer." With an arm beneath one of her knees, he fit his tip to her opening, and when she nodded, he thrust his hips, penetrating her fully and as deep as he could go.

"Ah!" As her maidenhead broke, a faint prick of pain went through her, gone in an instant, and then Gigi hooked her other leg around his, her heel digging into the soft flesh of his arse. "Oh, yes…" She moved into a more comfortable position as he stroked into her, slowly at first. "This is… This is…" Never in her wildest dreams could she have imagined what coupling with a man would feel like. Her eyes popped open, and she trained her gaze on his face. "Lovely!"

He grunted. "Hush, Genevieve, and enjoy. I'm nearly gone, but I'll strive to make this memorable."

Over and over, he pumped that beautiful shaft into her body until he found a rhythm and she was able to match it. "Good Lord…" One of her hands curled around his upper arm while the other she'd flung above her head to grasp at a wooden pole that supported the roof of the barn. Each consecutive thrust grew more powerful than the last, and each time they crashed together, her world shifted. All too soon, she was lost to wonder, the heat, the soft slap of flesh, to the scrape of his chest hair over her nipples. "Thomas?"

"Hmm?" His eyes were half-shuttered, the brown depths dark and unreadable.

"I need more. Give me all of you." A waver of uncertainty had entered her voice. She squeezed his arm. "If this bit of scandal is all we will share, I want to experience everything I can." For once they came back to reality, the gulf between them would return.

"In this, I agree." And the pace of his strokes changed as he went harder, faster, deeper. Quite frankly, he claimed her, even if he didn't know it.

As much as she wanted to deny it, this man who was an impossible match for her had the ability to send her existence tip over tail. It was all too much too fast, and she wasn't ready to fall in love, especially with a man she couldn't have, so she shoved away those budding emotions. As she let the sensations take over, tears welled in her eyes.

"I'm done for, Gigi."

As was she, for her body stiffened, and when she hurtled over the edge once more, she screamed and didn't care if everyone in the countryside heard her. Then she added more to her own ruination by slipping a hand between their bodies to touch the button he'd tormented earlier.

And she fell, pinwheeled into bliss once more where there was no sound or sight, just exquisite pleasure.

With a shout, Thomas followed her into that void. She clutched at him in a bid to hold him close, her body shaking and her core convulsing around his pulsing shaft. Warmth filled her as he ground his hips into hers to prolong the sensations for them both, but eventually, it was over. He collapsed on top of her, his breathing ragged in her ear. "Dear God, that was amazing," he whispered, and he held her close.

"It was." Gigi floated on a sea of feelings and emotions she couldn't pick through let alone separate. Instead, she wrapped her arms around him, kissed his shoulder, his temple, his cheek, before pressing her trembling lips into the curve of his neck. "Better than I ever expected." And she silently cried from the glory of her first bedding and how much she had enjoyed it. "Thank you."

"You are most certainly welcome." His lips glanced along the skin beneath her ear, and she rather adored the sensations that followed. "I enjoyed returning to the rogue I used to be, if only for an afternoon."

Eventually, she stirred, and Thomas rolled onto his side to face her. "Do you miss London and the life you had there?" What she wouldn't give to return to Town and do the society circuit. It was certainly better than rusticating in the country.

"In some ways, yes, I do miss London. It was more metropolitan, there was much more to do and see, and be entertained." When he grinned, the gesture reflected in his dark eyes. "However, I grew bored with living a life of vices and needed something more fulfilling."

"Which is how you became a vicar."

"Yes." He nodded, and she was hard-pressed not to devour his naked form with her gaze. It was enough to have him near. "While it took a long time to acclimate myself to the complete change in lifestyle and location, I have come to adore country living, to be grateful for the life I lead now."

"Interesting." Was that how he would spend the rest of his life? "What do his brothers think of you as a vicar?"

"They have difficulties understanding my calling, of course, but I could no longer knock about Town, spending an allowance from my father—and now my oldest brother." He shrugged. "We are all different."

"Is this living something you see yourself doing for the rest of your life?"

"I do." Nothing but honesty shone in his eyes. "It is what I was put on this earth for, I believe." He tucked an escaped tendril of her hair behind her ear. "I enjoy ministering to my congregation, to helping them and encouraging them. Someone needs to be a light in this world."

"And you are quite skilled at it." That was something she couldn't deny. "I just wish it wasn't the whole of your life, that you would take time for yourself, for you cannot help others if you are exhausted and beaten down."

"I understand that, and it's something I'm struggling with."

"I suppose everything is a learning process." Then the temptation got the best of her and she danced her fingertips along his shoulder. "Is there a lady in his congregation that you might think would be a good life mate?" When he frowned, she rushed onward because she needed to know. "Perhaps that woman who came calling the other day?"

"Miss Partridge?" Thomas blew out a breath. "I suppose she is a candidate, but I don't know much about her."

"Except that her character is sterling, and she doesn't have a scandalous reputation." Hurt stabbed through Gigi's chest even though she already knew *she* wasn't for him. "But I'm certain you will need to marry."

"Indeed, and the old vicar wrote to me, saying as much." As he shook his head, he shoved the fingers of one hand through his hair, leaving it in furrowed rows. "There are many things that weigh on my mind at present. My remaining unattached might prove a problem in the future."

Gigi tried to put his hair back into some semblance of style even though they still lay in the straw. "Then you *will* marry a member of your congregation." It wasn't a question, but rather an eventuality. As she spoke, she sat up and reached for her shift.

"Eventually I will. Perhaps more sooner than later, for the old vicar indicated he would be forced to pass my situation up to the powers-that-be."

"And they will force you to marry anyway, lest you lose the position." Reality intruded earlier than she'd wished onto their carnal bubble. "Once you take a bride, will you retain me as the girls' governess?"

"I cannot honestly begin to say. Everything would need to be weighed against everything else."

Which meant her being let go was a certainty. The ache in her chest intensified. She swallowed to dislodge the ball of emotion in her throat. "I am putting your reputation into danger as well as tainting the girls. I should never have taken this position, for in doing so, I'll destroy all of you." Tears welled in her eyes and spilled to her cheeks, prompting her to catch them with her shift. "Because you are too much of a gentleman, I shall make this easy for you. I'll return home and—"

"Stop." He put a hand on her arm to stay her flight. "I told you before to live for the moment and that is what I am doing, what you are doing. Right now." His gaze met hers, and he offered a small grin. "It is what we must do if we wish to continue… this." He gestured between them. "Do you agree?"

Did that mean he wanted more from her than this tryst? Gigi cleared her throat. "You also said do the most good where you can. I don't feel I've done that outside of teaching your nieces about real life."

"And I appreciate that about you." Thomas nodded. A wicked light appeared in his eyes. "Coupling with you is *quite* good, don't you agree?"

"Well, I thought…"

"Then don't think for a bit." Then he took the shift from her hand, tossed it away. "There is just this moment." He tipped her backward into the straw, took her wrists, and pinned them over her head. "So good, in fact, that we are going to seek pleasure all over again, because sometimes, a man needs to do something for himself that has nothing to do with his future or his living."

"As it should be." Though she was confused about where this afternoon would lead or where her own life was heading, she was soon lost in his kisses. All thought and worry flew out of her head as she applied herself to kissing him back.

There would be plenty of time to worry and wonder about everything later.

CHAPTER TWELVE

August 2, 1817

THOMAS RUBBED HIS eyes with his fingers then once more focused on the older woman seated across from his desk.

"I beg your pardon, Mrs. Camden but I don't see how *my* governess is any of *your* concern." And what was more, this visit was only one of many from a handful of well-meaning matrons within in congregation.

"Quite frankly, Mr. Alderman, there is a growing number of us who are concerned that the woman you hired for your nieces' governess is well… too attractive." When the woman nodded, her two chins jiggled, as did the feather in her bonnet. "Some of us even believe she is naught better than a harlot sent to take you from the church."

"Gammon!" His patience was sorely misplaced. "Miss Hasting is nothing but a proper governess. The children adore her. Yes, her teaching methods might be unorthodox, but they are effective, and I believe the girls will remember the lessons much longer than if they were ordinary." It wasn't anyone else's business.

The woman huffed. "Her teaching methods or how she fulfills her governess position are not what has the congregation inflamed."

Folding his hands atop the desk, Thomas bit back the retort he wanted to make. Instead, he pasted what he hoped was an understanding smile on his face and nodded. "Oh? What is, then? And do be advised that it isn't good for the spirit to listen and perpetuate rumors."

Mrs. Camden clutched her reticule in her lap and leaned slightly forward with worry and anticipation in her expression. "Miss Hasting has always had a… reputation for jumping into scandal with her eyes wide open."

"So do many people, and isn't that why we, as members of the church, should be examples of how to live?" He didn't care for gossip and rumors, and especially he didn't wish to hear Genevieve's reputation cut to ribbons. There was a certain amount of protectiveness in him for her, especially after the time they'd spent together.

"Yes, of course, however…" She lowered her voice. "Miss Hasting is a bit of a fast young woman. She's always seen fraternizing with men in the village, and there is talk of her having a new lover."

Heat crept up the back of his neck, and he hoped she didn't notice. "Is that so?" Dear God, had someone seen him with her? If so, his position would be in jeopardy. But to be fair, Gigi had been an innocent… until he'd taken that from her, so the theory she did have a lover wasn't true.

Unless those rumors referred to him.

"Oh, yes. It seems that girl just isn't content with putting forth a proper image or behaving herself." Mrs. Camdem nodded, as if that settled it. "And since she is your nieces' governess, there is every threat that she will pull you down into hell with her, Mr. Alderman. Something must be done, for there are far too many grumbles within the congregation."

"Meaning exactly what? And remember, gossiping is a sin, Mrs. Camden." No amount of wishing for patience could keep a note of annoyance from his voice.

With a huff, she wagged a finger at him. "Just this, Vicar. It would behoove you to marry rather more sooner than later to quell any rumors that might catch you up into their vortex." She stood and once on her feet, she inclined her chin while Thomas scrambled into a standing position. "Choose wisely, and choose a woman from your congregation, one that is winsome and amenable to most of your parishioners."

"And in the meanwhile?" But he *knew*.

"Sack the governess, Mr. Alderman, before she passes on her bad habits and questionable ways to your nieces." She marched to the door. "It will be a far greater sin to have the girls' reputations destroyed before they can even start, and them being a viscount's granddaughters too."

There was that, and it was a secret fear that lived at the back of his mind.

"Thank you, Mrs. Camden, for caring about us. I shall ponder seriously over your advice." He exchanged a speaking glance with the housekeeper as he passed her in the corridor while seeing the matron out. Once his guest had departed, Thomas blew out a breath and raked a hand through his hair. "Mrs. Traverse, please see that I'm not disturbed further this afternoon. I have a sermon to finish."

"Of course, Mr. Alderman."

"For that matter, where *are* my nieces?" There had been a significant lack of noise about the house for the past few hours.

"I believe Miss Hasting had them out to the pond for lessons and then a quick swim before returning home for tea." The housekeeper gave him a slight smile. "Is there anything else at the moment?"

"Unfortunately, no. There is nothing for me except to finish the sermon for tomorrow." With dragging steps, Thomas returned to his study and sat again at the chair behind his desk.

And stared at his sheets of paper spread out on the top while his thoughts ran amok.

What am I to do about Genevieve? Since her arrival into his life and the girls' lives, things at the vicarage had never been as content nor as indulgent. Penny and Lily were happy, for the first time in ever so long. They'd had a bad time of it with their parents and grandparents dying so horrifically, and their grins and laughter had been missing. But ever since Gigi, some of that had returned, and he couldn't fault her for that. She had been like seeing the sunshine after days of clouds and rain.

Additionally, his writing flowed into sermons as if he'd been given new life or a new hope. Never had he felt as energized or as expectant as he did now. Everything seemed brighter merely because of Gigi's presence. How was it possible that the advent of one woman could make such a difference? And a governess at that. To say nothing to the fact that the household ran with peace and efficiency. She'd had an effect on his staff as well, which boggled his mind.

Like with the geese and swans at the pond, humans flocked to her, wished to be in her close proximity. Did she give them a bit of calm as she did him?

He snorted. Well, calm when she wasn't driving him wild and making him as randy as if he were a green youth just setting out in London with his friends to chase skirts.

None of that mattered, however, if having her in his life for any capacity would continue to rile his congregation. As much as he dreaded having to talk to Gigi about leaving her position, he dreaded the fallout more from the church if he let her continue with being a governess. None of it was fair to either of them, but she also didn't deserve to have her reputation ripped to shreds merely out of an obligation to school his nieces. And if his trysts with her did remain a secret, that didn't excuse the fact they had already been as scandalous as people could be and had sinned so many different and delicious ways.

Beyond all of that, taking tea with Genevieve and the girls each day, as well as dinner some days of the week, made him feel more connected to them, made him feel like a father more than he had when he'd first taken the girls in… he felt like he had his own little family, and Gigi was the glue that held it all together.

Except it was her very sullied reputation that made her a horrible choice for a wife. At the last second, he tamped on uttering a gasp. Yes, he was well aware he needed to marry in order to calm the congregation—not that it was a good reason to marry—but at the back of his mind he'd wondered if he and Genevieve might be compatible in that regard.

Would she be a good wife? A good wife for a vicar? He didn't know, but there were obstacles in that path regardless. She wanted a titled man with a fortune and to be a lady of leisure, while he needed a woman by his side who would be as passionate for ministering to his flock that he was.

Yet…

It was an impossible situation, but he'd known that going in, and now with the veiled warning from Mrs. Camden and the no-so-veiled threat from the old vicar, something had to change, and perhaps that meant he needed to start with Genevieve. Unfortunately, that meant asking her to leave, and contemplating a life without seeing her throughout his days.

God help me.

"Uh, Miss Hasting, a moment of your time, if you please," Thomas said as tea concluded, and the girls trailed upstairs to their room for their hour of quiet time.

"Certainly, Mr. Alderman." There was a mischievous light in her eyes that would have ushered in expectation, but instead, it fostered unease in the form of knots in his belly. "Your study?"

"No, the parlor is just fine." Hoping he didn't cast up his accounts, he gestured to a low sofa where his nieces had sat during tea. For this undertaking, he didn't wish to have too much space between them. "Since this is a conversation of some delicacy, I'm going to close the door most of the way."

Damn the wagging tongues, though he trusted his staff implicitly.

"All right." A frown tugged at the corners of her mouth. "Is all well?"

"Honestly? No." There was no reason to delay. He moved across the room then shut the door three quarters of the way closed. The return trip to the sofa was accomplished much slower. Once she'd settled onto the piece of furniture, he sat as well. "I have been visited by no less than five concerned members of my congregation in the past day or so, and they have all been quite vocal in reminding me that I had a responsibility to my flock."

Confusion creased her forehead. "Meaning?"

Why couldn't the floor open and swallow him whole? "Meaning they want me engaged quickly, and…"

"And?" One of her blonde eyebrows rose.

Thomas cleared his throat. When his gaze met hers, his chest tightened. "And they are also unhappy that you are my nieces' governess. In short, it seems there are women within the congregation who believe you are too much a temptation and are only here to drag me into hell with you."

For long moments, she remained silent, then huffed. "Did you defend me?"

"I did, within the parameters that I could." He dropped his voice. "No one can know what we are to each other just now." What they could only be.

"Ah." When she wet her bottom lip, far too much interest shivered along his shaft. Emotions moved over her face, but they were fleeting, and he didn't try to read any of them. "You know, Mr. Alderman, it is a rather large failing of humans to judge others. Doesn't the Bible explicitly tell you not to do that?"

"I wasn't the one judging." Not liking her tone nor the over-bright look in her eyes, his chest tightened, and his muscles tensed. "I merely mentioned that some of my parishioners were, and I reminded them that gossiping was a sin."

Two spots of color blazed in her cheeks. "Those people don't know what sort of a person—a woman—I am, but why do they automatically think a *woman* is the downfall of civilizations or the breaking of a man?" She sprang to her feet, which necessitated him doing the same as Genevieve lowered her voice. "And might I remind you that you didn't exactly protest the things we've done together." Her eyes narrowed. "Men never face consequences while women are left watching their reputations and futures deteriorate around them. It's vastly unfair."

How could he rebut that when it was true? He should have called a halt to what was between them after it went past a few kisses, should have been a gentleman and begged off when she pushed for more, should never have initiated that coupling from a few afternoons ago. But all of that had happened, and now he needed to clean up the mess.

"On this, I agree with you." When she began to pace, he followed her movements with his gaze, trying to gauge how annoyed she was. "The society we live in is extremely one-sided. Men, especially those in the *beau monde*, are never held accountable. Barely a smack on the hand is all we receive, which is another reason why I wished to become a vicar. To try and help within the Church where I couldn't before, even with supporting causes that go against the grain."

"So then, why are *we* having this conversation?" She turned as she arrived at his desk, and then gasped with her eyes rounded. "Dear heavens, you intend to sack me for behavior unbecoming a governess, a lady of the *beau monde*, don't you? Because of those rotten gossips in your church."

"I…"

Anger flashed in her eyes. "Because you would rather protect your dratted image of a sinless vicar, protect your church full of Pharisees instead of defending me."

Her knowledge of what the Bible contained and how to apply it to the modern day had his respect for her rising and a grin tugging at his mouth. "While I also agree with you on that count, I did *not* defend them. It is a sticky wicket to keep a balance between my private life and my church life."

"We are both adults. There is no reason why we both cannot maintain a summer fling discreetly. No one would ever know, and they in fact don't know now." She shook her head. "When it comes down to it, you are a coward, Thomas."

"That I know. It's a failing of mine."

"Don't try to play charming and retiring." Genevieve crossed her arms at her chest. "You don't have any failings."

"I do, and they are things I am trying to work on."

She scoffed. "You are the nicest and perhaps most honest man I've ever known."

Well, damn. "I appreciate your faith in me, for sometimes I don't feel I am worthy to hold this position." How could he let her go? But if he asked her to stay, could he leave her alone? She *was* good for Penny and Lily. The girls' confidence had strengthened since Gigi came into their lives. "Which is why I'm ashamed to even have this conversation with you."

"Ah." A light of understanding appeared in her eyes. "You are under pressure to remove me from the position." It wasn't a question."

"As succinctly as possible, yes." He shoved a hand through his hair, which was rapidly becoming an anxious habit. "And in many ways, they might be correct, for you *are* a distraction of the most satisfying sort." Hoping he could charm her, he grinned, but her eyes narrowed further. "But knowing who you are and knowing how much everything has changed since your arrival, I think you should stay." What sort of nodcock was he? This would guarantee he'd lose his position and need to return to London—and his family—in disgrace. To say nothing of disappointing his nieces. Or even losing them if he had no living.

Surprise replaced the annoyance in her expression. "Why?"

"The good you are doing here far outweighs the bad that might come because of it." Of that he was certain. It was the rest of it that flummoxed him.

"You speak from desperation, or from your prick." When she

glanced down his body to linger her gaze briefly at the front of his breeches, he couldn't help but shiver. With a tiny sigh, she brought her focus back to his face. "Also, you are under pressure from someone higher up in rank. Retaining me is sheer folly, and you know it."

Thomas nodded, and with every word, his chest tightened and the urge to retch grew stronger. "They believe it looks bad for a youngish vicar to remain unmatched—"

"And you cannot align yourself with a woman who has made it a habit of chasing scandal without regret. A woman who doesn't wish to find herself tamed."

"Uh, I suppose." At least she said it so that he wouldn't need to.

"Ah." Genevieve pressed her lips together. "I understand. I don't agree, but I do understand, and perhaps it's important to show your nieces that doing the right thing for the wrong reason is sometimes the better part of valor." A trace of tears misted her eyes, made all the more evident in the sunlight.

Oh, God.

"I don't think there is any sort of valor involved in this decision." Every inch of him felt the coward she accused him of being. "I am in an untenable position."

"You are, and I wouldn't wish to exchange places for all the coin in the world." She brushed at the moisture on her cheek where a tear escaped. That tiny crystalline drop nearly had him throwing himself on his knees to beg her forgiveness. "As much as I adore Penny and Lily, I will, uh… remain here until such time as you can find a new, more proper governess," her voice caught and a piece of his heart flew into her keeping, "or until you select a suitably devout woman in your congregation to marry." Her chin trembled slightly. "After that time, I shall leave, but I refuse to go without saying goodbye to the girls. They have had enough loss in their lives already."

"Thank you for that small kindness." Admiration for her grew, even as hot panic welled in his throat. "Genevieve, please believe me when I say this isn't what I want." In fact, what he wanted was to take her into his arms, carry her up the stairs, and couple with her until this whole conversation was naught but a horrid nightmare. Once she walked out of his door, he had the feeling he would never see her again, even though she lived just over a mile from the vicarage by way of the meadows.

She tossed her head then raised her chin with all the stubbornness he'd come to realize about her. "Don't make this worse than it needs to be." A note of false brightness clung to her voice. "We both knew what we had was temporary at best. A summer tryst. It passed the time and allowed me to explore more of the carnal side of myself." Though she shrugged, she looked away, pretending faux interest in a bird just outside the window. "Perhaps I was led here for the girls, to give them a bit of confidence and strength to be able to begin the next phase of their lives. I thought it was important to show them there is more to being a young lady than letting society tell them they can only become a wife or mother." Then she swung her attention back to him, and he pressed a hand to his chest where the worst of the pain was. "Perhaps I provided you with the same, but now my time is finished."

"Just as life has seasons, so too does the time with the people in our lives."

"So it is." As she made her way through the room toward the door, she wiped away another tear. "I hope that in the course of you trying to please everyone around you, that you realize you deserve happiness too."

What sort of monster was he? "Gigi, please wait." More than ever, he wanted to kiss her, hold her, comfort her, but it wouldn't amount to anything definitive, for she wouldn't dare wish to align herself with a country vicar and he couldn't afford to marry her.

"You know why I shouldn't." Her voice was hushed, graveled with emotion. "I'm going upstairs to read and then retire early. I suddenly have a megrim and don't wish to be disturbed."

"What of dinner?"

"I'll take a tray in my room if my head is better."

"Very well." Thomas nodded even though everything in his brain screamed at him to stop her, that he needed her for more than just a summer's tryst. "I will keep the girls busy and ask them to stay away. I wish you a good rest."

"Take them out to the pond. They like it there, and even though we already had swimming time today, they can run off some jitters and tire themselves out." Her smile was a watery affair at best.

"I will, and I will say a prayer for you."

"Thank you." Then she was gone, fleeing from his study with a stricken expression on her face as if he'd ordered her to a convent.

As if his knees would no longer support him, he sank onto the nearest chair, planted his elbows on his knees, and then buried his head in his hands. This was the beginning of the end, and suddenly he couldn't bear to contemplate what that future would look like without Gigi's light and personality.

And yes, her penchant for challenging him at every turn as well as her siren's call.

CHAPTER THIRTEEN

August 3, 1817

THOUGH TODAY WAS Sunday, Gigi didn't feel that she could sit through Thomas's sermon this morning without wanting to burst into tears. It was silly and stupid to feel as if she were in mourning, for it was just a governess position, and one she hadn't wished to take anyway.

But the gist of it was she would miss him as well as his nieces. Those little girls had managed to worm their way beneath her skin in such a short period of time that she could almost imagine them belonging to her, that she would see them grow into young ladies and help get them launched into society.

Except, that wasn't to be.

When she'd told Thomas last night she'd been suffering from a megrim, that wasn't a lie. Perhaps it had been the sun from swimming yesterday with Penny and Lily or perhaps it was the fact she hadn't much of an appetite since that coupling with the vicar in the barn, but more likely it was the sick feeling that had accompanied the ache in her head knowing she would soon lose the paying position she'd had for little over two weeks.

I'm a failure.

What would Mia say? What would Cora? No doubt one of

them would lecture her while the other would tell her she had an obligation to the family to find a new position.

Instead of going downstairs to breakfast, she made certain the girls were outfitted for church, then she told them of her headache and that they would need to attend with their uncle. Protests abounded, but eventually they understood she wasn't playing and bowed to authority. Which made Gigi feel even worse, for she didn't enjoy taking orders in her life either.

Once Thomas left for the church with his nieces, she dressed herself, drank a cup of strongly brewed tea, told the housekeeper she would be back in the afternoon, then departed on the walk toward her family's manor house. The one saving grace? It was once more overcast with the fat, gray clouds portending rain at some point in the day.

In that, the weather perfectly suited her mood, and she mentally berated herself for acting the ninny over a man. An unavailable man at that. But the confusion persisted as well as her megrim. Surely, she shouldn't feel so emotional over the vicar after such a short period of time. Yes, they'd fallen into scandal, and yes, she had probably pulled him into it when she shouldn't have, but it was only a physical relationship. There weren't any feelings involved. They'd given each other pleasure and that was all.

Wasn't it?

Shortly after gaining Andover Hall, Gigi found her mother in the morning room.

"Good morning, Mama."

Surprise lined the other woman's face as she set down the book she'd been reading. "Genevieve! How lovely to see you." Then concern swept in. "Is all well with you? It is half-past nine. You should be attending services."

"Don't lecture me about that, Mama. I am simply not in the correct mindset." Without being invited, Gigi took a seat at the table where her mother was enjoying a breakfast of tea and toast. "Besides, I needed some time away from the vicarage and thought perhaps visiting you and Papa might be just the thing to sweep away my doldrums."

"What of your charges?"

"They are with their uncle, and he is perfectly capable of looking after them, even while he's in the pulpit. I'm certain they will behave." Though, whether the girls would actually follow through with that was another matter entirely. "Besides, Sundays are my days to attend to my personal life."

"I see." Her mother took a sip from her teacup. "How are you finding your position otherwise?" She glanced at Gigi. "I had one of my friends in for tea the other day. She told me there are some scandalous rumors circulating about you."

When are there not?

She blew out a breath. "People tend to glean much entertainment tearing down others." That was all she would say.

One of her mother's blonde-gray eyebrows rose. "Are they not true? Have you curbed the tendency to act without thought?"

Heat slapped at her cheeks. "I don't know about that, but whatever you have heard through the gossip mill, I'll wager it's wrong."

"Good." Her mother nodded. "I was afraid when you took the governess position that you would find Mr. Alderman far too handsome and a temptation."

Well, that fear certainly came to pass.

"He *is* easy on the eyes." There were simply some secrets a woman needed to keep and hoard them to herself. "His nieces are lovely, if a bit wild around the edges."

"Just as you were at their ages," her mother said with a laugh. "And continue to be."

"I cannot help who I am."

"Oh, don't I know it? I long ago stopped hoping you would grow into a proper lady, but I can still dream." Then her expression hardened a bit. "Though if you *are* chasing scandal, you could possibly be destroying the vicar's plans for the future." Even though Gigi made a sound of protest, her mother continued. "There's talk he wishes to marry, and soon, and will choose an eligible party from his congregation. I should hope you don't get in the way of that."

"Of course I won't, for I'm only a mere governess, correct? I shouldn't use my position to try and find a match for myself, hmm?" Where the devil did that come from? She hadn't changed her mind about marrying titled man with a fat bank account, and certainly there weren't any of those men about in a country village or church.

"You have said yourself many times over there aren't any interesting men outside of London." Speculation jumped into her mother's eyes. "Has someone caught your fancy?"

"No, of course not." An image of Thomas danced across her mind's eye, of him smiling so that the delicate skin at the corners of his eyes crinkled. When the image shifted into one of him naked with concentration on his face as he thrust into her body, a wave of heat washed over her. "Most of my time is spent with the girls."

"As it should be. You are at the vicarage for one specific purpose. I hope you won't let anything distract you, but once the vicar finds himself engaged, I'll wager he'll ask you to leave, for having a youngish, pretty woman underfoot might cause difficult feelings."

Gigi waved a hand, for it wasn't anything she'd hadn't already discussed with Thomas. Without going back to London, her own chances of finding a match were slim. "Do you think I should apply to a position in Town? Perhaps that would broaden my opportunities of finding a husband." It had certainly worked for her sisters, yet the men they'd wed were far from being rich. "Or should I remain close to home due to Papa's health?"

"Only you can say that for yourself, but it is nice that you're close."

"Except Papa doesn't know who I am most days." The thought of that made her stomach drop every time.

"That doesn't mean you shouldn't visit. I fear he won't have much more time on this mortal coil." Sadness pooled in her mother's eyes.

It was another sure sign that things were changing, and it left a raw ache in her chest. She needed a distraction, and soon. "Is he up and around this morning?"

"Not that I'm aware. He is sleeping still, and I didn't wish to disturb him." Her mother frowned. "Perhaps you should lower your standards regarding men, Genevieve. Titled and well off is a tall order, but there are many lovely men who possess decent enough incomes you can set your sights on, especially if you wish to have babies of your own. You aren't growing younger."

"I haven't decided if I wish to have children; I'd rather have the man for a few years before that closeness is taken away by the responsibilities of being a mother." None of this talk helped her sort out her confusion. "Are you pleased that Mia and Cora married poor men?"

"It is not for me to puzzle out the mysteries of the heart. I just hope your sisters get by in life without struggling and with plenty of happiness and love. At the end of the day, that is what everyone is searching for—love."

Which brought her thoughts back 'round to Thomas. How *did* she feel about him? Physical attraction and the carnal pleasures to be found in his arms were one thing, but had her fondness for him stemmed from merely that? And she absolutely couldn't contemplate a lifetime with him, for he was a vicar and that would mean she would be forced to be someone else entirely.

I just cannot do that… even for love.

And she simply wasn't in love with him, so at least that was one saving grace.

"Where are my sisters?" Perhaps they would provide the distraction she needed at present.

"Emmaline and Anne are puttering in the garden. I believe Nora is in the drawing room with her handiwork."

Gigi nodded. "I'll just pop in on them for a few moments

before walking back to the vicarage."

"At least stay the day and have luncheon with us. It is much quieter around here without you to maintain the chatter." Only then did she see how frail and tired her mother truly was. "I miss the spirited conversations you and sisters used to have."

Her heart trembled. "I promise more frequent visits." And if Thomas were serious about choosing a bride, she would have nothing but time on her hands.

A few minutes later, she found Nora in the drawing room, not working on embroidery but utilizing her sketch pad and her charcoals.

Gigi made certain her sister could see her before she spoke. "Hullo, Nora. How are you?"

Since Nora couldn't—or wouldn't—speak verbally, they had all been working with a tutor that came in once a week to teach the language of the signs that had been invented by Benedictine monks. Mia had made good on the promise and engaged the tutor soon after she'd married her viscount.

She followed the verbal inquiry with the appropriate signs made with her fingers.

Her sister's eyes lit with happiness. "Gigi!" The verbal utterance sounded more like a labored grunt, and the sign for her name always made Gigi smile. *What are you doing here?* Though the signing took a bit for not only Nora to get out but also for Gigi to interpret, she felt nothing but relief for the gift of communication.

"I didn't wish to attend church services. Instead, I thought to spend time with you and the family." She sat on an ottoman in front of her sister, so Nora could see her lips and fingers as she signed. "How are you?"

Well enough.

"That's good." Gigi gave her a smile.

Are you enjoying being a governess?

"It is certainly more work than I first thought, but there are moments of fun, and I truly adore the vicar's nieces." If she were asked to leave her post due to his engagement, the absence of the girls would leave a void in her life. "The position doesn't leave much time for a personal life or men, even if Mr. Alderman is quite lovely." Though she'd managed to slip away with Thomas well enough. Another round of heat went through her cheeks, for she would do it again in a heartbeat.

Then Nora frowned and peered closer into Gigi's face. *You should pursue that man.*

"What man?"

The vicar. I can feel you like him more than you ought, so chase him, if he makes you happy, especially if you find fulfillment in his arms, in his bed… and even more so if you love him.

For a few seconds, Gigi stared at her sister. "I don't love him."

Nora became agitated. *Poppycock! Your whole face lights up when you speak of him and your eyes twinkle. That only happens when you feel truly connected to a man.*

"What? That doesn't mean I love the vicar." When Nora didn't seem convinced, Gigi gasped. "*Do* I love him? Surely not." Was that the reason for her confusion and overly emotional responses? "He isn't the sort of man I want for myself, for my future. It won't help Mama or Papa—"

Nora huffed. Her fingers flew as she talked. *It isn't your responsibility to save the manor. Nothing matters except being happy and proud of who you are.* She again peered into Gigi's face. *Something is different about you.*

"I don't think so." Could a person perish from burning heat in the cheeks?

There is. I can tell. I know the secrets my sisters keep. Nora nodded. *Cora had a secret too, once, and only I knew.*

"What was it?" She had no idea her sisters kept secrets from each other.

I cannot tell.

Gigi frowned. Could she share something as private as what she and Thomas did together?

Be honest. Do you love him?

"I…" That wasn't an easy question to answer.

The truth. Life is too short to lie to yourself. Nora flashed a smile that completely transformed her features. *Set everything else aside. Dig down into your heart of hearts, your very soul. If you were not with the vicar, if you never saw him again, how would you feel?*

"I don't know." How *would* she feel? "He's as handsome as sin and we have…" She dropped her voice. "We have gotten into scandal a couple of times; though it was glorious and everything I ever dreamed of, he has already said I am not the type of woman he can marry." Yet he'd been willing to put his position into jeopardy by keeping her on as his governess.

Did that mean something?

It's there in your eyes, Gigi. You love him. Almost desperately.

"But it's been only two weeks. How could anyone fall so fast? I don't believe it." Yet even though she denied it, she felt *something* there, something that went beyond the carnal.

Love doesn't need a timeline or rules. It just… is.

"But I'm too… bad. I cannot be the kind of woman he needs in a wife." The knowledge sent pain stabbing into her chest.

Nonsense. If he loves you, if he truly believes in what he preaches, your past—and his—won't matter. Nora's fingers fairly flew. Obviously, she'd studied the hand gestures, and Gigi had trouble catching up. *And you are a lovely person, Gigi. You just refuse to see it for fear that being good won't be fun.* She gestured her closer. *Enjoying intercourse and appreciating a man's body doesn't make you bad. Never let anyone tell you otherwise.*

"Oh, Nora, I want so much to believe you." For years, she'd thought there had been something inherently wrong with her because she adored chasing scandal over propriety. "In some ways, I wish I was a proper lady like you and our sisters. Then he might see me not as a sin but as… a treasure." Though her finger signing was slower than Nora's, it got the job done. Why did the views of the Church make her feel less than?

"No!" The word was spoken audibly and with definitive power. Nora shook her head. *God made man. God made woman. God created physical love. The end. Anyone who says otherwise can go hang.*

Despite her scattered thoughts, Gigi snorted with laughter. "Oh, I love you so much, Nora." She came off the ottoman to embrace her sister. "I hope you're right about me being a treasure, but I rather think I'm a hopeless cause."

Nora huffed. *Talk to him. Make him see reason.*

"I will certainly try." Though he was stubborn and would err on the side of deflecting the most gossip.

LATER THAT AFTERNOON, Gigi returned to the vicarage with her stomach growling for tea, and her heart dancing with anticipation to see Thomas.

Except the vicar wasn't in residence. Instead, his friend Lord Grantford was waiting in the parlor, and according to Mrs. Traverse, he'd been there already thirty minutes. The vicar had sent word he'd taken his nieces visiting a few people in the area and to not except him until dinner.

"Then why is the viscount cooling his heels here?"

"Who can say? But he's requested tea. You might as well share it with him." Then she continued along the corridor toward the kitchen.

Moments after stepping into the parlor, Gigi greeted him. "Hello, Lord Grantford."

He scrambled to his feet. "I'm afraid you have the advantage over me." His voice was a low baritone, not like the addictive tenor of Thomas's.

"I'm Miss Hasting."

"Ah, yes. The governess." He gestured to a low sofa. "Please, join me. I've been waiting for Thomas, but he has been out for a while. I don't wish to return to my lodging house just yet."

"I see." She settled onto the sofa, and when he sat in a matching chair nearby, the scent of sandalwood wafted to her nose. Much different and not as intoxicating as what the vicar smelled like. "It's always lovely to have company."

He nodded as he roved his gaze over her person. "You are just as Thomas described."

"Is that a good or a bad thing?" How interesting he'd talked about her to a friend. Was it merely in passing or did it mean something more?

"That is, perhaps, not for me to say, for I tend to err on the scandalous side, and I chase women who also have that in common." His grin was this side of cheeky, "But he also said you have been instrumental in bringing his nieces to heel."

Gigi snorted. "I don't know about that. The girls merely need a trace of discipline instead of having the spirit taught out of them."

"I enjoy how outspoken you are, Miss Hasting. Too many women repress their own spirits in order to fit in with society. After a few years of that, they become copies of each other, and who wants a woman who is the same as every other?"

His line of thinking surprised her, and she smiled. "Thank you. It is rather how I've seen life as well." Suddenly, emotions beset her she hadn't counted upon. "Not many men can appreciate that."

"Then they are blind as well as nodcocks."

"Thank you." She lowered her gaze to her hands in her lap.

"Thomas told me about the fete. He has expressed an interest in perhaps doing a few events with Miss Patridge and then dancing a set with her that evening."

Another jab of hurt went through Gigi's chest. "Good for him." Then she frowned. "I suppose for all his talk, he's taken the hints and veiled threats to heart."

"So it would seem." Lord Grantford's gaze was on her when she looked up, but he didn't have the power to stoke her awareness like Thomas did. "I suspect he does wish to marry, and soon. It will go a long way in halting the rumors and speculation."

"Speculation about what?"

"You, Miss Hasting."

"What?" Flutters went through her lower belly. "Why me?"

"According to the men in one of the taverns, they have two-to-one odds that our good vicar will succumb to the temptation you represent soon, if he hasn't already."

"Ah." She hoped her expression gave nothing away. "First, I find it rather disconcerting and slightly rage-inducing that the general populace thinks that a woman with any sort of pleasing looks is naught but a siren. And secondly, what sort of Church people are these who perpetuate such rumors that can damage both parties?"

Even if they were true.

"I like the fact that you aren't afraid to defend yourself, Miss Hasting."

"Someone needs to. There is a definite lack of honor and gentlemanly manners around here." Crossing her arms at her chest, she huffed and glared at the viscount. "He is quite welcome to the incomparable baker, Miss Partridge." Was that too snippy? Too revealing?

Lord Grantford's lips twitched. "They do make a handsome couple."

"Perhaps, though I'm not convinced they will suit." And if the subject matter didn't change soon, she would become a watering pot in front of this man. When had she ever let emotions rule her being so much?

"Why not?" Had Thomas not told this man everything? "They seemed quite cordial the other day."

"Oh, I don't know. Just a feeling." His grin continued while he shrugged, and it was far too charming. "By the by, I am attending the village fete in four days. I'm coming as Thomas's guest, but will you come as well?"

"I haven't decided yet. Why do you wish to know?"

There was a gleam in his eyes she didn't quite trust. "I would like it very much if you did, for I have enjoyed talking with you, and in the event you haven't noticed, I am also unattached." When he winked, a faint tremble moved through her chest.

"Oh." Ordinarily, it would have thrilled her to have another man interested in her, but now? It was still pleasing, but it made her nervous. She didn't want that life any longer. The thought of perpetually flirting, teasing, leading a man on with kisses or promises had grown stale. In fact, she only wanted Thomas.

Yet it was too late for that. Not that they ever had a chance beyond what they'd physically shared. What did that mean for her future?

There was no way to know, and she needed to perhaps have a different plan. Slowly, she nodded. "Perhaps I will, and I *would* like to further our connection, Lord Grantford." Offering him a smile, she rose to her feet. "We can wish Thomas, er, rather Mr. Alderman, well if he announces his impending engagement at the fete."

Surely such a relationship wouldn't go so quickly? Her heart squeezed with hurt.

"Excellent!" The viscount stood as well. "After the week concludes, I would like to host a trip to London for you, if that's not too bold. I'd like it very much if we could attend a few society events together, for there are many possibilities opening up before us, don't you think?"

"Perhaps." Though she smiled, it felt wobbly at best.

He nodded. "Thomas has hinted to me you wish to align yourself with a wealthy, titled man. I am that, and I am captivated by a woman who isn't guided by rules."

"So you are." Could she settle for this man since she couldn't have her first choice?

"And handsome enough." He scooped up her hand and brought it to his lips where he kissed the back.

An unexpected chuckle left her throat, and a hint of heat infused her cheeks. "I won't stroke your ego and agree." If she couldn't have the vicar, why not let the viscount court her? She would have everything she'd ever wanted in a man, in a life, and there was nothing wrong with that.

Right?

Except… Her chin trembled as Lord Grantford released her hand. Perhaps she'd been a fool, for she was a ninny after all. She couldn't be certain, of course, but she might be falling in love with Thomas, or at least the idea of him. Never had she expected falling in love to hurt so wretchedly, and the near constant ache in her heart was not pleasant. He'd made his position clear, so she shouldn't waste those emotions on him. Was taking the next best thing the clear choice? It might be her only choice now, and the last chance she would have of making a decent match.

Was coming here to be a governess so that she would meet the viscount part of God's plan? And if so, what of the connection between her and Thomas?

Why the devil is life so confusing? And why had her sisters not told her of this part of romance?

"Well then, who needs tea when a man has secured the promise of a lady?"

Oh, he was charming enough and handsome. There would be no end of fun and excitement with him, but he wasn't Thomas. He didn't wear somber clothing or have a dimple in his left cheek when he grinned a certain way, nor did he set her aflame with a mere look or inflection of his tone.

At the last second, Gigi stifled a sob. "Then I should retire to my room. The megrim I've been suffering from demands rest. Please either wait for Thomas to return, or show yourself out." Then she fled upstairs, and barely reached the refuge of her room before the tears began to fall.

The question that remained now was would she give up gracefully or fight for him?

CHAPTER FOURTEEN

August 6, 1817

T *HE LAST THING I want to do is attend this fete.*

But it was what he had to do if he were to find a suitable candidate to begin courting. An engagement couldn't happen unless a courtship did first, and in order for *that* to take place, there needed to be a connection, a spark.

The past four days had been strained and awkward at best between him and Genevieve. While he hoped she might have defied him once more, she took great pains to avoid him at all costs. Two of those days, he was hosted for dinner at the homes of his parishioners. The other two were at home, and though Penny and Lily kept up a steady stream of conversation, their governess had remained uncharacteristically quiet with downcast eyes and a demure attitude.

During the days, she taken care to either keep the children in the attic-turned-schoolroom or they took lessons abroad in the countryside with picnic lunches and a change of clothing in the event they went swimming if the afternoons were stifling.

There had been no chance for flirting, casual touches, stolen kisses, or even a conversation that might relieve the tension between him and Gigi. Beyond that, he missed her smiles, the mischievous light in her lake-blue eyes, and the way she would constantly remind him that his way of thinking wasn't necessarily the correct one. Additionally, he missed the sound of her humming when she sat in the garden and thought she was alone. Often, those melodies wafted through his study window when he worked on his sermons. He missed her floral scent, and rarely did he catch snatches of those perfumed ghosts, for she rarely ventured out of her room if she was in residence. He even missed the evenings when they both sat in the common room reading books on vastly different topics, when he would read passages from his works, and she would return the favor.

And he didn't know how to fix their relationship beyond going back on everything he believed in or betraying his flock.

"Come and join in the game of croquet, Vicar."

The sound of a woman's voice yanked him from his musings, and it took a few seconds for Thomas to focus on the redhaired woman. He nodded and offered a polite smile. "Thank you. Perhaps I will in a bit." Ordinarily, he didn't mind the attentions of eligible women in his church, but today, the scrutiny and interest grated over his nerves.

"Don't linger too long else the games will end for luncheon," she said as she passed his location with a simpering smile and a flutter of lashes beneath the brim of her bonnet.

Tamping down the urge to grumble, Thomas glanced across the wide expanse of the village green where long tables had been set up. Crisp ivory cloths covered the surfaces, and the edges of them danced in the errant summer breeze. Settings had been laid; the sunlight sparkled on the silverware and glass, and the appetizing aromas of savory things wafted to his nose even at this distance as various villagers worked to arrange platters of food along the middle of all the tables.

"Now why would a man so sought after try to hide himself beneath the shade of these trees when he could be out there, flirting as he played croquet?"

He jerked his head around as Lord Grantford joined him,

looking as fresh and pressed as if he were about to step out onto a dance floor in London.

"I am simply not of a mind to mingle just now." If it sounded far too grumpy, so be it. Thomas tugged on the knot of his cravat. "This gathering has made me quite nervous."

"Ah, well, that is understandable," his friend said as he clasped his hands behind his back. "I'll wager your current confusion has nothing to do with the fact you are at odds with Miss Hasting."

Merely hearing her name sent awareness prickling over his skin. "It is for the best." Though he remained wildly unhappy about this latest turn of events, he couldn't go back on the decision. He had responsibilities, and he was a changed man besides.

"Yet you aren't doing the pretty with Miss Partridge either," the viscount was quick to point out. "She is fetching today in that sky-blue dress."

Thomas flicked his gaze across the lawn to where croquet was being played. Miss Partridge was one of the participants, and indeed, she was lovely in the dress, and the matching ribbon in her brunette tresses called attention to her high cheekbones and slender neck. "Indeed, she is." While Miss Patridge was lovely and wholesome and everything he should want in a potential wife, she wasn't Genevieve, but the woman he wanted was the one person forbidden to him. "I expect the congregation is waiting for me to formally pay my addresses." The knowledge sent a stab of pain through his chest. If he chose Gigi in defiance merely to please himself, it would practically spell an end to his living. He would be replaced by someone else, someone better who had a stronger will, who would be more able to follow the Bible's dictates.

"Oh, indeed, and why wouldn't you? Everything about her screams proper and demure," Grantford said with a touch of amusement in his voice.

"Yes." Feeling far too glum, Thomas nodded. *I've failed at everything.* He owed it to himself and his congregation to toe the line and maintain the proper image of a leader. How could he expect his flock to follow the teachings found in the Bible if he didn't?

"Sometimes, Thomas, I rather believe you are the biggest nodcock I've ever met."

"How do you figure?" It was enough to shake him from his musings to focus on his friend's face. "I am truly struggling."

"There *is* an easy answer to that." Grantford nodded. "Miss Hasting is summer personified today, wouldn't you say?"

Despite himself, Thomas followed his friend's gaze. His world seemed to tilt, for Genevieve was easily the most beautiful woman he'd ever known. Clad in a dress the color of daffodils, she stood out among the ladies who wore white and ivory. Her golden hair gleamed and almost made her resemble an angel. While she talked and laughed with a few younger ladies, his heart stuck in his throat.

Why couldn't she act that free and genuine in his company?

He blew out a breath. "You know why anything with her is impossible for me."

"I know you are an idiot of the highest order. Miss Hasting is a wonderful woman, and since you are too set in your ways, I think I might try my luck with her."

Jealousy speared through his chest, and the ache was felt in his heart. "You should. She is part of the *beau monde*, and you are apparently everything she wants from a match." Grantford was much better suited for her. "Let me wish you well. No doubt you will be quite happy together, and if you don't treat her well, you will answer to me." It was the least he could do for her. Swallowing hard around the ball of emotion in his throat, Thomas nodded. "Do make certain you seat yourself near her at luncheon."

"Perhaps I will." The viscount frowned. "If I were you, though, I would decide what it is *I* truly want before too long. There will come a time when you cannot go back, and a chance might be forever lost. It has been my experience that good women will not wait around forever."

And she already told me she despises weak-spined men. The urge to cast up his accounts grew strong. "How can I, in good conscience, decide with my heart and soul when knowing that will muck up everything I have worked for in the past few years?"

"I didn't think you for a dunce, Thomas." Grantford shrugged. He huffed. "The question should be how can you not? No doubt life will work itself out, and the people who have their noses out of joint can get glad in the same face they were mad in." He clapped a hand on Thomas's shoulder. "At the end of the day, it *is* your life. Congregations and livings come and go, but who you have at your side is forever."

"It is much too soon, isn't it, to fall in love with a woman who is still much a stranger?" he asked in a soft voice. "Doesn't it take time and copious days spent in each other's company to necessitate a fall?"

The viscount snickered. "The fact you need to ponder the question indicates you have already tossed your hat over the windmill for the woman."

"Then that makes this all the more pathetic."

"Oh, indeed. Much like a drama played out on a Drury Lane stage."

Thomas shook his head. "It doesn't matter. There are others I must think about above myself." As he continued to watch Genevieve, who now talked and laughed with his nieces, who looked every inch like summer in their ruffled white dresses, Miss Partridge moved into his sight. She waved, gestured at him, then pointed at two chairs at the end of one of the tables. Clearly, she wished for him to sit next to her for luncheon. With a bit of a feeling that he went to his doom, he nodded. "Well, I should mingle. It's what a decent vicar would do."

"Perhaps, but you are also a coward."

"Yes, so I've been told before."

"It would behoove you to listen, then." Grantford had pity in his eyes as he regarded him. "I hope Miss Partridge proves everything you hope for." He dropped his hand. "And when Miss Hasting and I are taking London by storm, I'll be sure to write to you. No doubt she'll prove quite the adventure between the sheets."

Thomas bristled. He curled a hand into a fist. Though he wanted to punch his friend in the nose and hear the satisfying crunch of cartilage, he refrained from violence. "I refuse to dignify that with a comment."

"Ah, then that's as good an endorsement as any." Grantford chuckled and he grinned as he glanced at Thomas's fist. "Enjoy luncheon. I certainly will." Then the viscount took himself off. In short order, he reached Genevieve's side, and immediately she flashed him a wide grin while the girls ran toward his location. With his golden head bent close to hers, it was already evident they were a good match and had much in common. No doubt he would give Gigi the life Thomas could only dream of... if he wasn't a vicar.

Dear God, why does it hurt so much to see her obviously happy? Shouldn't I want that for her?

But why couldn't she feel that with him? Why wouldn't he let himself have that with her?

"Hullo, girls. You both are quite lovely today." And that was all due to Gigi's influence, for it had been she who'd helped them to pick out their outfits. "And it's quite a fine day for you to run about, hmm?"

"Uncle Thomas!" Lily ran up to him, then threw her arms about his hips. The purple satin sash about her waist matched the one in her dark hair. "Will you sit with us at luncheon? And there *is* a May pole but it's not even May!"

He couldn't help but grin over her wonder and enthusiasm. "Of course I'll sit with you. I plan to share the table with Miss Partridge as well."

Penny frowned. She fussed with the yellow satin ribbon around her own waist where a posey of wildflowers rested. "Might we sit with Miss Hasting instead? She is ever so much fun, and she knows loads of stories."

"I rather think you should be with me just now." He infused a brightness into his voice he didn't feel. This were exceedingly fond of Genevieve, and they would be devastated when he had to let her ago. "Once we come to know Miss Partridge better, I'm sure she'll be just as entertaining."

I hope.

"It's a good thing for you to spend time with Miss Partridge. She's a lovely young woman, don't you think?" For he might as well make inroads into courting the young woman.

All for the sake of a damned reputation and image, of keeping this living, which was much like pulling a lie about himself. What did it matter who he chose as a wife? Why the devil was he content letting a few gossips and an old vicar decide his fate?

"Her cake tasted like paste." Lily was nothing if not honest. She tugged on his hand. "I want a lemonade."

"So do I," Penny agreed with a shake of her head. She glanced across the lawn. "Who is the man talking to Miss Hasting?"

He didn't need to look to know. "My best friend, Lord Grantford. They make a fine match, don't you think?" The ache around his heart had grown in intensity.

Penny's frown continued. "One of my friends says you will marry Miss Partridge." She glanced up at him with worry in her eyes. "Are you?"

What to tell her? "Uh, I'm not certain yet. There are many things to consider."

"No!" Lily stamped a foot. She popped her hands on her little hips in much the same way he'd seen Genevieve do. "You should marry Miss Hasting."

"Miss Hasting is ever so lovely." Penny tugged on his other hand. "She is much better than Miss Partridge, and her voice sounds like a song."

Didn't he know it?

"Miss Hasting is your governess, but Miss Partridge is someone I am considering a courtship with, and she is a member of the church." Not that the girls would understand all the reasons he *should* choose Miss Patridge.

The girls exchanged a glance, and even a blind man would know what that meant.

"Don't you think Miss Hasting is pretty, Uncle Thomas?" Lily wanted to know.

"Of course I do, but—"

"Miss Hasting feels like a mother." Penny peered at him with expectation.

Thomas frowned. "What does that mean?"

She huffed. "When Miss Hasting hugs me, it's tight and squishy. Miss Patridge's hugs don't feel like that."

Lily nodded. "And her eyes don't smile like Miss Hasting's do."

Well, that was true. He'd noticed that as well.

"And…" Penny said as she tapped a forefinger on her chin. "Miss Patridge doesn't know about floating flower crowns on the water when you want to speak to the people who have gone before." Her expression suggested it was an affront to show ignorance in the subject. "She said it was scandalous to say so, and that I shouldn't bring it up again. She said people can't talk from heaven."

That was true also, but there were many different ways to honor loved ones. It seemed Genevieve had given the girls back their hope in life. Their sadness from months before had dimmed. Not forgotten, of course, but they weren't incredibly focused on it every day.

"People are different, and there is nothing wrong with that."

Penny stared at him as if trying to puzzle something out. "You should marry Miss Hasting. She makes all of us happy. Lily and me like having her around."

"Sometimes, pet, adult business and interactions are far more complicated than that." Taking them both in hand, he led them across the lawn toward the tables. "Luncheon will begin soon; we should find our chairs." As he guided them to where Miss

Patridge stood, his gaze accidentally collided with Genevieve's. She talked with Lord Grantford not far away.

He grinned and inclined his chin in greeting. She acknowledged it by giving him a nod, but her smile was more dull than usual, but then the fleeting few seconds she'd exchanged with him were over, for she responded to something Grantford said, laughing with him and then moving off toward a table at the opposite side of the square.

Dear God, how can I survive losing her?

Chapter Fifteen

Throughout the luncheon, Gigi picked at her food. Though the company was pleasant enough, and Lord Grantley certainly paid her enough attention that it should have made her happy and ready to drag him off to a private spot, she couldn't seem to let herself relax enough to enjoy the day.

"You are quite distracted, Miss Hasting, even though I'm doing my level best to engage you in conversation and pull you in with my charm." Amusement threaded through the viscount's voice.

"I apologize for being poor company, Lord Grantford." With a sigh, she glanced at him, for he didn't deserve her fractured interest. "My appetite has been poor the past few days, and outside of keeping watch on the girls, the afternoon is rather dull." She breathed in deeply then let the air ease out. "To say nothing of the fact that I don't belong here."

"At the fete?"

"No, the village, the community, within the church." Waving a hand to encompass the happy chattering gathering, she sighed again. "Do you ever feel as if everyone around you is committed to something you have either no idea about or no interest in?"

"Many times." He broke off a piece of a biscuit and held it to her lips until she took it into her mouth. "I have never enjoyed bucolic life. Why Thomas insists upon it when he could be back in London, having the existence he was born to is beyond me."

"Perhaps he wanted more than being merely the son of a viscount." When she sought him out with her gaze and watched him talking and laughing with Miss Partridge, a part of her died inside. "Now he'll marry a woman with connections and is well liked in the village, who understands the importance of the Church and religion, a woman suited to his life as a vicar."

"Now that I find difficult to believe." When he met her gaze, Gigi gave him a half-hearted smile. "Perhaps you feel out of sorts because the countryside doesn't fully do justice to your soul, and it certainly doesn't highlight you as a woman."

"But that's just it." She laid a hand on his arm, and when his muscles tensed beneath her fingertips, she immediately withdrew. "I *should* be comfortable here. It's where I live, where my parents live." Was it boring here? Yes, of course. Would she rather be in London where there were constant entertainments, glittering jewels, and pretty gowns? Also, yes, but sometimes life didn't work like that.

"Humans, I think, can survive many things, especially when there is a reason to do exactly that, a motivation of sorts." One of his golden eyebrows rose in question. "Do *you* have that, Miss Hasting?"

Heat went through her cheeks. "You refer to Thomas."

"You brought him up; I did not." The viscount lowered his voice even though there was enough conversation and laughter swirling around them that it was doubtful they'd be overheard. "If I may be so bold as to posit that you wouldn't appear so upset about our good vicar taking a bride if you didn't have feelings for him."

"That is another thing that is so confusing," Gigi admitted in a choked whisper. "I have known him two weeks. That isn't enough time to form a tendre, let alone fall in love."

"Ah." He leaned close so that his lips brushed the shell of her ear. "Yet it's enough time to chase scandal with the man, to allow him certain… liberties?"

The heat from her cheeks migrated throughout other portions of her body. "Sometimes there is an undeniable connection between two people, and it is folly not to act on it." If it made her sound deranged or depraved, so be it. "Does that equate to love? I rather doubt it. Infatuation, perhaps, but since Thomas's life is his own, he can court and marry anyone he wishes, especially if she is better suited to his work than I am."

And it made her heartsick all over again.

"I see." Lord Grantford frowned. "Have you spoken to Thomas about how you feel?"

"Of course not. He is stubborn and has specific views of what the Church expects from him." She gasped at the pain around her heart. "I cannot compete with that; neither can I change his mind." Across the green, Miss Partridge was apparently doing her level best to monopolize Thomas's time while the girls sat on either side of him with matching scowls. Obviously, the woman hoped to set herself up to be his wife. Many of the older people in the congregation were already happy with the prospect. Seeing her with him only solidified that in their minds. "I can bear witness to this no longer." As she shot to her feet, the viscount stood too.

"Where are you going?"

"I don't know."

A wicked light had entered his eyes. "Would you like company? I've been told I am a rather wonderful distraction."

For a moment, Gigi knew a bit of indecision. In the past, she would have been overjoyed that such a handsome, titled man had shown an interest in her, and for scandal, to boot. Yet now, all she could think about was losing Thomas. "I appreciate the offer. Truly, but…"

He nodded. "I understand. Perhaps once you put the heartbreak of the vicar behind you and you realize there is still much that life can offer you? When you realize that many of us consider you beyond worthy already?" After he dug into a pocket of his jacket, he withdrew a card. "Write to me at this address. I will drive here, scoop you up, and carry you back to London for adventures, both carnal and otherwise."

That tugged a grin from her, and she felt almost her old self again. "I appreciate that. Thank you." As she tucked the card into her reticule, Gigi left the village green at a brisk walk with no particular destination in mind.

FIFTEEN MINUTES AFTER she'd taken refuge in the back garden of the vicarage, the sound of her name in *his* voice sent gooseflesh racing over her skin.

"Genevieve? Are you out here?"

Of course he had followed her. It was both comforting and annoying. With a huff, Gigi turned about to face him. "What do you want, Thomas? Won't Miss Partridge be disappointed you chased after another woman?"

"Miss Patridge has no bearing on my life at the moment." There was an intensity to his eyes she didn't trust, but it made her anticipate the meeting, nonetheless. "I wanted to speak with you, for you have proved elusive the past four days."

"Whose fault is that?" Refusing to feel guilty, Gigi went deeper into the garden.

Fruit trees laden with growing apples as well as other ornamental trees blocked out some of the sunshine, while a hedge formed the rear boundary of the space. Bushes and other shrubberies hosted berries as well as birds who enjoyed feasting on said berries and the flowers within. Beneath the lifted arms of the trees rested a wooden bench along with a gardener's table. The man who kept the garden tidy came to the vicarage a couple times a week, but he'd left the tools of his trade on the tabletop: pail, gloves, trowel and spade, a couple of smaller pots containing cuttings of various plants and flowers. Between the rear of the space and the back door of the vicarage, many groupings of flowers, bushes, and shrubs made pleasing arrangements to wind through when one wanted a peaceful interlude.

"While I will admit to being much of the issue, you have to take some agency as well." He followed her through the garden, the heels of his boots scraping against the crushed shells and gravel that made up the path. "But talk we must."

Though every part of her wished to race into his arms, if he only wanted her for the physical release, if he considered her too tainted by scandal to remain in his life, Miss Partridge was welcome to him. "What is there to converse about? You said everything you had to say. There is no room for rebuttal. That leaves me with nothing."

"I can appreciate how you might view the problem." Tension brewed in the air between them. How could he stand there so calm and composed when her belly was in knots, her thoughts jumbled, her world crumbling because she wasn't good enough to either remain with the girls as their governess or be with him in any other capacity than a quick toss in the hay?

For lack of anything intelligent to say, and detesting the silence, she blurted, "You certainly seemed comfortable at the fete. No doubt you charmed your way through the afternoon and will do so tonight for the dancing."

He snorted. "I'm not one for dancing any longer, but when I lived in London, it was part of my everyday schedule, especially during society events." His voice was so low, she barely caught the words. When he turned her head and found her gaze, stark longing lit those depths for the space of a few heartbeats. "However, effective dancing depends entirely on the right partner."

"Have you found her, then?" Did he regret the time they'd shared and was too much a coward to admit it? Did those couplings mean nothing? *Do I mean nothing to him?* Hot panic welled in her chest. She wanted to flee but remain in his company, for already their time together was limited.

"That remains to be seen, for there have been other things clouding my mind of late." Though he didn't make a move to close the distance, there was no mistaking the desire in his eyes.

Why was he such a puzzle to read? "Miss Partridge seems lovely. I hope the girls take a liking to her."

"Ha. At present, both Penny and Lily do not care for her, because she isn't you."

"Ah." A curl of pleasure unfurled in her stomach, but she strove to keep her expression impassive. The girls were loyal, it seemed. "Perhaps they shall come 'round. When, uh, will you begin courting Miss Partridge?" A waver entered her voice, and she despised that weakness. It didn't matter to her what he did with his life.

Did it?

"As soon as possible, I'd imagine. Especially since I expect a visit from someone higher in the Church than I to check on me." His Adam's apple bobbed with a hard swallow. "I am not pleased with the timeline."

"I don't blame you." It was as if they chatted like strangers, never going deeper than congenial conversation. Not seeing him or being with him for four days had left her feeling quite ragged about the edges. "Ah, Lord Grantford has offered to host me on a visit to London, should I wish to try my luck in Town after I'm let go from my position here."

"Well, he's a good sort, and he is everything you are searching for in a husband." When he met her gaze, there was a frantic need in those stormy gray depths that called to something in her. "The two of you will make a wonderful match."

"What if I don't want that any longer?" she finally whispered, circling the edges of the truth. Tears welled in her eyes. "Is this where you and I will end, then? This horrid talking about things that don't matter?" She drew in a shuddering breath. "Besides, being here alone with you is not proper, and don't you want that above all? It's why you created the rift between us in the first place." There. At least some of what bothered her was out in the open.

"Damn, Gigi, how can you say that?" He shoved a hand through his hair. At some point, he must have misplaced his gloves and top hat. "*We're* not proper. Never have been since the moment you stepped into my home."

She shrugged. "You are the one who told me I wasn't good enough, that I am somehow tainted and too scandalous to be in your life." A tear fell to her cheek. "And it's quite confusing *because* you are here, talking to me, when you should be with Miss Partridge."

"I left her with the girls, hoping they would bond. Told her I had a parishioner to attend to and would return in an hour." Thomas nearly spat out the words. "But I don't wish to speak of her right now."

"Then you should have thought about that days ago." She raised her hand in annoyance, thinking to slap him, but then thought the better of it. "In fact, you should never have taken me on as governess, for so much has happened between us, how can you expect me to forget it?"

"I don't." His eyes were stricken. "For I won't, but—"

"But you retain this nodcock idea of wedding the perfect woman worthy of the Church." She shook her head as a tear fell to her cheek. Why couldn't he see that no one was that? That even Miss Partridge was probably not what she appeared? "I wish you every happiness in life, Thomas, but we cannot continue to see each other. It is too painful."

"I agree in theory." His nod was curt. "Will you go to London, then?"

"Yes. In fact, after your sermon on Sunday, I'm going to pack my things and return home. We both require that distance between us." Tears sounded in her voice. "I'll spend a few days with my family and then write to Lord Grantford. I imagine once I come to know him better, he and I will have great fun together." And she scrubbed impatiently at the moisture on her cheeks.

"Bloody hell. No!" Thomas quickly closed the distance between them. He gripped her upper arms, gave her a little shake which forced her to look into his eyes. "Grantford is not who you deserve."

"Who *do* I deserve then? You have certainly rejected me, in part due to rumor and my own behavior—with you." Hot annoyance circled through her being, and her voice broke. "Well, I am done being told the only good woman is a proper woman or being shown that I'm only worth a convenient place for your prick."

"That isn't it... I never meant to..." A string of emotions went over his face, but in the shade, it was difficult to read them.

Gigi waved a hand. "Don't trouble yourself. We were never meant to have forever together, but what we shared was—"

"Bloody hell. Stop." He caught her hands in his. "Perhaps I *am* a coward after all, but I want—need—to give you a proper goodbye."

"I would like that as well." She stood there, peering up at him, the words she should have said sitting on the tip of her tongue. If she uttered them, they would make her far too vulnerable, and could usher in more hurt. "Thank you for the time we did have together..."

"Damn." Thomas took her into his arms and kissed her soundly. It was a hard and unyielding embrace, and it gave her back the life that had ebbed from her over the past four days. "Please remember me, Gigi. I fear I am making a huge mistake," he said between kisses that set her blood on fire and heated every inch of her skin.

"I could never forget you." With all decorum forgotten, she returned his kisses with her customary enthusiasm. Soon, she was as breathless as he.

"To hell with it. What is one more sin?" Before she could protest, he propelled her through the garden, through the plants and shrubberies and beneath the trees, until the worktable prohibited further movement. With a grunt, he lifted her, rested her arse upon it. Potted plants and the bucket of implements tumbled from the table and crashed to the ground with dull thuds. "Thank heavens I gave the staff the rest of the afternoon and evening off to attend the fete. We are much alone." When her legs naturally splayed, he settled between them, and cupping her face in his hands, he set out to kiss her senseless.

Oh, goodness, he will drive me mad.

One more taste, one more drink from his lips, one more time having his body crash against hers…

How can I walk away from him?

"This is wrong, and according to you, I am wrong for wanting it." Yet she slid her fingers through the hair at his nape in an effort to tug him closer, for his kisses were as intoxicating as wine. "You smell so good."

"And that yellow dress is lovely on you. It's quite a flattering color." Never did he cease in his intent to claim her. He treated her to deep, drugging kisses that imprinted his very essence into her brain, much like what she'd probably done to the swans and geese at the pond. When Gigi would have giggled, she couldn't, for that would mean stopping the kisses, but the embrace simply wasn't enough. God help her, she wanted all of him, needed to be with him, so she urged him closer.

"I need more of you than this position will allow," he whispered against her lips.

"I don't believe I told you nay to any of it."

With a growl that sent another wave of awareness over her, Thomas snatched her off the table and maneuvered her between the trees without breaking a new string of kisses. As her back connected with the wall, he deepened the embrace.

In the course of two weeks, she had met a man who'd turned her world upside down, who challenged her and wouldn't let her boss him. She'd fallen for his nurturing soul and spirit, had shivered into obedience by looking after his nieces, and in the gray depths of his eyes, she'd been shown a glimpse of a future she'd never realized she wanted… and now couldn't have.

How can I be expected to just forget him?

As tears welled again, Thomas continued to kiss her. He took away her tears, made certain she'd keep his memory alive and etched upon the very chambers of her heart, tried to convince her within that torrid embrace that this final coupling would be enough. And she was inclined to agree, except with each breath, panic and hurt came to life inside her chest, behind her ribs, and around her heart.

"Thomas, please." What? She couldn't very well beg him to choose her for everything that mattered when doing exactly that would destroy his life. He didn't deserve that, and she didn't want him to resent her.

"I know." As he nipped and licked her lips, he slid his hands to her thighs and hefted her up as if she weighed nothing. "Dear God, you are a fever in my brain, and in this moment, I hope never to be cured." Propped against the wall, her center aligned with his bulging erection, and he groaned even as she wrapped her legs around his waist. "We shouldn't do this."

"But we must. To end it." Despite her resolve not to fall victim to emotions, Gigi's heart broke again, into finer pieces than it previously had, for this was the last time she would see him, unless she accidentally came across him while visiting her parents. *I can't think about that right now.* "Show me that if circumstances were different, you would choose me."

"As if I haven't shown you such already." With eyes haunted by sadness, Thomas yanked down the bodice of her dress and the petticoat beneath, buried his face between her breasts, palmed them, and suckled the nipples until she moaned and squirmed against him.

Time was of the essence. If the housekeeper or a curious maid came back early, heard them, and decided to investigate, there would be hell to pay, and she wanted this joining more than she'd ever wanted anything in her life.

"Did I at least make a difference in your life?" She gave herself up to the feel of him against her, that sold wall of his chest, how the heat of him called out to her. With a sigh, she twined her arms about his shoulders. "Have I made you think any different-ly?"

"Was there any doubt? I have never met anyone like you."

"Oh." Yet she wasn't good enough for forever. Hot tears rose in her throat; they cut off her next words. This was exactly why she didn't believe in love. It did nothing to a person except give them a lot of heartbreak and those feelings of euphoria wouldn't last a lifetime anyway. "Just kiss me." So she would remember and ultimately forget.

"Gladly." Hefting her up again and pressing her harder into the wall at her back, Thomas kissed her as if she held the last drop of water and he needed it.

Despite the tears that fell to her cheeks, Gigi returned his kisses for all she was worth; she wanted this moment in time to last. When he delved a hand between them through yards of fine lawn to stroke his fingers along her sensitive folds, she very nearly tumbled into release sheerly from the emotional torment. "Yes, please more," she softly encouraged, and held him all the closer.

"I don't know if I can last through extended foreplay." Then his hand shifted as he wrenched at buttons to his frontfalls. "I want you, to feel you around me." And then the tip of his hardened shaft slid against her flesh, and she shivered.

"I want that too." A moan escaped her throat when that wide head glanced over the opening to her channel. Undeniable need coursed through her veins. She tightened her legs about his waist, dug the heel of a slipper into his buttock to encourage him forward, and the dear man didn't hesitate. He thrust once and deeply until he was fully seated. "Thomas!" Pleasure tingled through her being, but she died a thousand deaths to know this was final.

And goodbye.

"You feel amazing."

"Exactly that." And it was far too sad. Not wanting to see the pity in his eyes, Gigi closed her as she wriggled into a more comfortable position and held him tight. "I wish things were different."

"Yet we both knew going in this was impossible."

"The risk was worth it." But the loss was devastating.

With a half-cry, half-groan, he pushed into her with long, powerful strokes.

"Oh, yes!" Being joined with him was too much. All she wanted to do was cry, and soon she would break apart, yet she couldn't help but enjoy this one last coupling. His thrusts grew more frantic. Harder, deeper, faster he moved his hips, as if he sought to be one with her just as she did with him, and she worked to match his rhythm. Would it be declaring defeat if she changed everything about herself to become the woman he thought he wanted? Not knowing, but refusing to give up who she was merely for a man, Genevieve bucked her hips in time to his frantic movements. Even as her tears fell, for those precious few seconds, their breathing, their coupling, their souls aligned.

Everything was perfect.

"Damn, I'm gone." With a soft cry of protest, Thomas apparently fell over the edge. Warmth spread into her core, the very last of him she would ever share, but she didn't care, for she went too, hurtled there by a swift pinch to her own nipple.

The hard release smacked into her like a rogue wave, and a low-pitched scream left her throat, which quickly turned into soft, whimpering cries, for this was the end. And there was nothing she could do about it except collapse into him, clinging to his neck as if he might disappear.

"What am I to do, remembering you and knowing you are gone, knowing you are with another woman?" Her whispered words were so low and choked with tears, but she didn't care. It was how she felt.

And he could stop it all if only he changed his thinking... or she hers.

It was the devil of a puzzle, or perhaps a test from God.

Did that mean she'd failed, or had he? Not knowing, she burrowed her face into the crook of his neck as Thomas held her tightly against his chest, telling her with his body what he couldn't with his words, or so she wished to hope. Once more he protected her, and she sought that solace and peace, that shield from all the changes of life she'd fought so hard against.

How silly of her to think she could avoid them.

She didn't know how long they stayed like that, but her breathing had long returned to normal, and her tears had somewhat dried.

Eventually, he released her and lowered her to the ground, kept hold of her until she found her footing. There was suspicious moisture in his eyes as he peered down into her face. "Thank you, Genevieve." He dropped a kiss to her forehead. "I wish you a good life and much happiness with Lord Grantford. You deserve that."

"And I hope you find everything you need with Miss Partridge." With hot panic rising in her chest, Gigi cupped his cheek—the last time she would ever touch him. "Your flock is fortunate to have such an upstanding and devout man leading them." She pressed her trembling, kiss-swollen lips together as she held his gaze while tugging her bodice back into place. "I'll return to the fete first, and I would appreciate it if you came along a bit later."

"Of course." He nodded and avoided her gaze as he fumbled with the buttons of his front falls.

"The girls will no doubt need some time alone, so I'll bring them back here for a rest and refresh. I will tell them my goodbyes and then escort them to you for dinner. In the morning, I'll leave for my home. No sense drawing this out."

I'm not strong enough for this. All the lives that were trapped in upheaval simply because she wasn't the proper society miss everyone expected her to be.

CHAPTER SIXTEEN

B Y THE TIME Thomas returned to the fete after he'd put himself to rights, his mind felt as if it would explode for all the thoughts churning through it.

Once more, he'd proved himself a rogue by coming together with Genevieve in a semi-public place as if he hadn't sense in his brain, as if he were little better than the man he used to be, but where she was concerned, nothing made sense except being with her. When he'd seen her talking and laughing with his best friend, something had snapped within him, and jealousy had consumed him in a hot tide.

Yet he still had no right to claim her or dictate her time, so he'd had no choice but to tell her goodbye the only way he knew how, the only way it would mean anything to both of them. That emotional connection, that one last coupling had nearly broken him, and he didn't think he could survive the coming Sunday knowing it would be the last day he would see her.

Luncheon had concluded and the tables were being moved to one side of the village green, for dancing would take place on the other side before dinner was served later that evening. Another round of croquet had formed not far from that location, while couples and groups had decided to stroll through the village, perhaps in search of shade or shopping, but he immediately found

Gigi with his gaze, and she appeared to be quite upset as she talked animatedly with Miss Partridge.

As he quickly walked toward them, Thomas finger-combed his hair into some semblance of a style, and prayed he looked presentable. Another sweep of the area didn't reveal Grantford, so perhaps the man had returned to his lodging house. At least he wouldn't try to spend more time with Gigi.

"What has happened?" he asked as he joined the two women—the one he couldn't have, and the one society deemed he must settle for.

"Oh, Thomas, the girls are missing," Genevieve said, with watery eyes and fear etched through her face. "Miss Partridge simply let them wander off."

"What?" Shock hit him like a punch to the gut. He rounded on the other woman. "I told you I had something urgent to attend to and asked you to watch over my nieces. Why would you let them run away?"

Miss Partridge blew out a breath. "Those girls are hardly docile or proper. There is no telling them what to do or hoping they will act demure or sit quietly." She shook her head, rested a narrowed gaze on Gigi. "Of course, knowing who their governess is, I cannot be surprised, for the children must have modeled their wild behavior after her."

Both he and Gigi gasped at the barb.

He cleared his throat. "In all honesty, my nieces were wild long before I engaged a governess for them, but that is beside the point." When he briefly met Gigi's gaze, saw the concern in those blue depths, he lost a piece of his heart to her. She so obviously cared about the girls, the difference between her and Miss Partridge was like night and day. "However, I did leave the girls in your care. Where did they go?"

Miss Partridge gestured vaguely to the east of the village. "I would have no idea. They were babbling something about picking flowers to make wreaths."

"Perhaps they went to the meadow not far from the vicarage," Gigi said as she shaded her eyes with a hand and looked in that direction, as if she could see the area from her present location.

"It's a good possibility. We'll start there."

"I would be happy to go with you," Miss Partridge purred with a hand on his arm.

In some impatience, Thomas shook off her touch. "You have done enough. I'll go alone."

While the woman pouted, Gigi huffed out a breath. "I'm going with you."

Worry collided with panic and the other jumbled emotions currently stuck in his chest. "If you had attended the fete as the governess you were engaged as, the girls wouldn't be missing now," he snapped at her, for if something were to happen to his nieces…

What sort of man was he to leave the girls—his own precious nieces—in the care of a stranger so that he could couple with Gigi like a half-crazed rabbit? He'd only thought of himself and the needs of his body, had let emotions have at him without stopping to think about his actions or to pray over the problem with God.

I have failed as a man and as a vicar.

"Ah, so then according to you and most of your church, I'm to be seen and not heard, act docilely mute, I shouldn't mingle within the community, nor should I talk with people who are higher in rank than a mere governess, regardless that I'm a baron's daughter." A fair amount of ire threaded through her voice, and her eyes flashed blue fire. "I am allowed my own life and my own interests, especially when your nieces were in your company this afternoon because you wished for them to come to know the *paragon*, Miss Partridge."

A blush stained the other woman's cheeks. "I apologize for not taking better care of them—"

Gigi snorted. "Well, we cannot *all* be governesses, can we?" Then she pushed her way past Miss Partridge.

Well, damn. Thomas gave Miss Partridge a half-hearted smile of apology. "Stay in the square in the event the girls return here. I must go search for them." Then he loped after a very angry Genevieve, but not so quickly that he couldn't appreciate the swish of her hips.

When he finally fell into step beside her, he grunted. "None of this would have happened if I hadn't engaged you as a governess."

She blew out a breath. "If you hadn't, those girls would have trampled all over you, disrupted your sermons, and generally been branded as heathens or hoydens, depending on who you talked to."

"Then why the devil weren't you watching them today? If you think yourself a governess who is unparalleled, you should have been with them." No matter that he knew the words were hurtful, he couldn't stop them from vomiting from his mouth.

With a gasp, Gigi paused and rounded on him. "How dare you." She poked a forefinger into his chest. "I brought Penny and Lily out to the fete because you were too busy acting like a damned politician, charming your way through your parishioners. Then when you remembered you were responsible for the girls, what did you do? Use them to get close to a woman you wish to court."

"I don't want to, but it's what I need to do in order to keep this living!" If he couldn't get on the other side of his emotions, the girls wouldn't be found, and he would inadvertently wound Gigi too deeply to heal.

"Ah, because that is the most important thing in your life." She looked at him as if he were a bug on the sole of her shoe. "Even more important than the people around you. Message received." Hurt reflected in her eyes, and the delicate tendons in her throat worked with a hard swallow. "Perhaps you should pray to God for help; you certainly don't appreciate me being here in any sort of capacity except the carnal."

Heat went up the back of his neck. "That isn't true." Though he understood the frustration and annoyance that had put her needles out, nothing had changed. Not really. Then he cleared his throat. "I apologize for what I said. Because I wished to couple with you, tell you goodbye in a way that I thought would make an impact, I left my nieces with a veritable stranger." The truth of his own actions was crushing. "It is my fault as much as yours."

She gave a curt nod. "At least you can see that."

"Gigi, listen to me." He laid a hand on her arm, and she immediately retreated to break their connection. "Being a vicar *is* an important part of my life. No matter who I take to wife, they will need to square with that."

"I understand, I truly do, but your position—the Church—cannot be the *only* thing in your life." Despair clouded her eyes, then tears welled to obscure any other emotions. "Knowing you are so high above us, that you practice at being so pious, makes it terribly difficult for the rest of us to live up to, and eventually it *will* isolate you."

Every moment they lingered to argue possibly meant the girls might have found trouble, but his pride was now engaged. "What the hell does *that* mean?"

"What do you think?" Gigi propped her hands on her hips, but that only served to draw his attention to that part of her, and his mind wandered to how it felt when he'd had his hands beneath her skirts and trailing his fingertips along her silky skin. "You are looking for perfection in a woman; you assume there is such a thing. You want a woman by your side who will make you look better in the eyes of the Church, who doesn't have flaws, someone whom everyone will adore, a woman who will never have her own opinion or interests or flaws." She shook her head. "There is no such thing, and why would you want any woman to parrot back your views or never challenge you?"

"I never said that I wanted perfection." How she'd come by such a theory, he couldn't know, but it only added to his confusion.

"Perhaps, but you implied it, and that's the same thing." Tears continued to well in her eyes. "It's how you have made me feel, as if I am less than everyone else, as if I will *never* be worthy enough to mean anything to you beyond a quick tryst."

Dear God, is that what she truly thinks? "It wasn't my intention—"

Gigi held up a hand to stop him. "Life is messy, Thomas. It doesn't matter if you have faith or believe in God or have impossibly high standards. Life is what it is and what it will always be. It's messy and scattered and frustrating and sometimes sorrow filled." A tear fell to her cheek as she shrugged. "Having faith can be comforting, sure, but you must understand that trying to figure it all out *while* living it is part of being human."

"That makes sense, of course, but I'm terrified of returning to the man I was before I became a vicar. The man of vices and sins. A man God would frown upon."

A snort came from her. "Then your version of God is askew. Does not God love everyone, regardless of their pasts?"

"Yes, but—"

"You assume that life is either one way or the other. It's not true."

He frowned. "Meaning?"

She sighed. "You labor under the assumption that you were bad or evil before as a viscount's son *because* the Church told you that you were. Now you are trying to be good and without sin, which not only is it impossible—for no human is that—but it removes so much of your personality you become lost in the masses. The Bible refers to followers as sheep because they will move en masse after one leader or another. And, nothing against the Church, but you are all blindly following someone else's dictates or interpretation of what the Bible truly means while trying to strive for some skewed view of perfection, of what a member of the Church *is supposed* to be. It's exhausting and you will never attain it."

Shock slammed into his chest as if she'd delivered a well-aimed punch. "No one can live up to that image."

"Exactly." A tiny grin curved her highly kissable lips. "If you continue like this, the girls will soon find they can never live up to those ideals. They will be gutted because they'll think the people they are will never be good enough—for you, for the woman you marry, for the Church, and possibly for the men *they* might marry." A waver entered her voice. "It's a horrible life thinking that way. You should live in a way that will serve as an example of truth for them. It is in the imperfections that we all find love and acceptance."

With the ache intensifying around his heart, Thomas stared at her as if seeing her for the first time. "I had no idea I was damaging so many people by perpetuating a lie inadvertently."

"At least you know now." Gigi met his gaze, and the moisture-spiked lashes that framed her blue eyes spoke of vulnerability. He wanted nothing except to hold her, comfort her, but to do so would prove folly, for he had already told her goodbye. "I don't begrudge you the church or the sermons. If that is your calling, then so be it, and you have a knack for orating." This time, her grin was genuine.

Heat went through his chest. "Thank you."

Gigi nodded. "If you enjoy being a vicar, that's all to the good. I just want you to understand there *is* good, joy, love in the imperfections. There is life there, interest too. And in being imperfect, in *trying* to live a good life, you do the best you can with what you have. You have faith the rest will follow, but you cannot continue to hold everyone around to such a high standard, because everyone will fail, even with grace."

How had she become so wise? "And that should be where the Church comes in, where imperfection lies, because we are all born of sin, and if we were already like Christ, He wouldn't have needed to die for us." Damn it all to hell. He stared, stunned, at her and the realization he'd just made. Or rather the one she'd smacked him upside the head with.

Have I unconsciously done that?

Had he used his position to stop living his life over a flawed view that he had to be so holy that he couldn't enjoy anything or anyone? So that his past would be erased, when all along he should have used that as an example of overcoming? That he'd isolated himself in an effort to be… perfect, when that was never attainable anyway?

What a nodcock I've been.

"I am so sorry, Genevieve. Please forgive me." He wanted to throw himself onto his knees and grovel until she relented, but he needed to find his nieces first. "For everything."

"Thank you." She wiped at her tears. "It is what it is. Once we locate the girls and make certain they're safe, I will pack my things instead of waiting until after Sunday. You and I are too different and always will be such."

Panic rose in a frantic wave throughout his being. "We aren't."

"Oh, Thomas." Another few tears fell to her cheeks. "We are, and I think you know it."

"No! It was flawed thinking, and—"

"Stop." Slowly, Gigi shook her head. "I live in the moment, go where the wind takes me, do things that make me happy, that make me feel wanted, and I don't worry about whether others consider those things scandalous or wrong."

"And there is nothing horrible about that, but—"

She made a sound that was much like a stifled sob. "Life is too short to always live how others wish us to. It's maddening, and in doing that, I do my best. I help others. I care for those less fortunate, but I do it because *I* want to, not because some man in a pulpit told me to do those things to redeem my soul." She paused while wiping away tears. "Life just… is. But there must be balance. If there is not, the mind will go insane."

"But I…" It didn't matter, for Gigi had turned away, gone ahead of him. She wasn't listening any longer. Besides, he needed time to think on everything she'd brought to his attention, make certain he had indeed been wrong. He needed to pore over texts, reexamine them with this new realization, and if he found that supporting evidence…

Dear God, could he possibly have a life with her as his wife?

The closer they came to the pond where Gigi had taken the girls several times before, the more the frenzied honking of geese reached his ears. "Penny! Lily!" Relief twisted down his spine, for the girls squatted at the edge of the pond as the sunlight sparkled on the ripples in the water. He ran to the pond and reached them the same time that Gigi did. "Why didn't you tell someone where you were going?"

I could have lost them simply because I've been distracted by their governess. Yet he would lose her regardless.

Before either one of them could answer, Genevieve pulled them both into her arms and held them close to her chest. "You gave us a fright." Her voice shook. "Don't ever do that again." As if her muscles would no longer support her, she collapsed to her arse with her legs folded to the side. "I was so worried."

"Miss Hasting, you're squeezing me too tight," Lily complained as she wriggled from Gigi's hold.

Penny frowned. "Why were you worried?"

Thomas sank to his knees on their other side. "Because Miss Hasting cares about you." He swallowed the ball of emotion lodged in his throat. "I do, as well, so when you ran away from the fete without a word, we were afraid." At the water's edge, the pair of geese were in the process of waddling out of the pond.

"Sweetheart, why did you come here so abruptly?" Gigi asked of Penny, who twisted the stems of daisies in her fingers.

"Lily and I wanted to pick flowers, but Miss Partridge said that was messy and hot." The little girl blew out a breath. Annoyance went through her expression. "So we came by ourselves."

"Why?"

The youngest girl put a daisy chain into Gigi's lap. "We wanted to make wreaths like you showed us."

Penny nodded. "So we could talk to Mama and Papa."

Thomas exchanged a glance with Gigi. "Why?"

Lily poked his shoulder. "We want to ask Mama if she would

be upset."

"Why?" Gigi bounced her gaze between the two girls. "Why do you think that?"

Penny smiled. "We want Uncle Thomas to marry you, so you can be our new mama." She glanced at him. "Miss Hasting said we could always talk to Mama and Papa whenever we wanted."

"But Uncle Thomas doesn't want her, Penny," Lily said with a frown and watery eyes. "My friend Sarah said he wants Miss Partridge. She isn't as fun as Miss Hasting."

"Oh, dearest." Another trace of tears welled in Gigi's eyes. "There is much more involved in romance than being fun." With a poorly stifled sob, she gathered the girls to her again. "I'm glad you are both safe."

Penny pulled away. "We weren't in danger. The geese kept us company." When she moved to the water's edge and tossed in her flowers, Lily did the same.

Thomas got to his feet and stood with them, vowing to never let them out of his sight, but when he glanced backward at Gigi, his heart squeezed. The pair of geese had come up to them. They made low honking noises of either welcome or inquiry. One of them nibbled at the hem of her dress while the other came close enough that she stroked its neck. When she dared to kiss the goosey head, his world tilted, and he lost another piece of his heart to her.

How could anyone be considered bad when animals trusted them so much? When children did? When his staff did? How could he have doubted her when he felt alive and encouraged each time she was near?

As she murmured soft words to the geese, he pressed a hand to his chest.

Dear God, have I been wrong this whole time and sat in judgment of her when I am just as imperfect?

There was much to ponder. "Come, girls. Let's go home. This day has been exhausting. I need to be with my thoughts and discover when I toss the things that don't matter away what I'm left with and what exactly I need."

Penny snorted. "You talk funny, Uncle Thomas."

"Perhaps I do." He stooped down and hugged his nieces, those precious little girls he was entrusted to care for, but he couldn't do it alone. Then he picked up Lily and set her on his shoulders. Too embarrassed to look at Gigi, he said, "I'll make tea, and we shall have many sweets, because today is a special day."

For he knew now, more than ever, he was hopelessly in love with Genevieve Hasting.

I have been a fool.

Could he pull out of it, convince her of his sincerity? He smiled up at Lily, and then an idea formed. Perhaps he would enlist the help of the girls, and anyone else. He needed Gigi in his life in all the ways that mattered, and this time, he wouldn't allow convoluted views and half-baked thoughts to distract him from his purpose.

CHAPTER SEVENTEEN

August 9, 1817
Landover Manor
Bedfordshire, England

GIGI LAY ON her side and trained her gaze on the open window where a gentle summer breeze flirted with the lace-edged curtains. The heat had broken a couple of days ago when a storm had blown through, leaving the area drenched in sunshine and comfortable temperatures.

It had been three days since the scare over her missing charges, three days since that last, intense coupling with the vicar, three days since she'd packed her belongings and moved back to the manor house. She had failed as a governess, of that there was no doubt.

All she had for her time at the vicarage were wonderful memories and intense heartbreak.

And she'd failed at everything else too.

For the past two days, she'd kept to her bedchamber and spent copious hours crying. All three sisters had attempted to come in and talk with her, but she sent them away saying she wasn't ready. Then her mother had assumed that she was no doubt repenting at leisure where she'd jumped into hasty scandal.

To which Gigi had politely asked her to leave her alone as well.

Did she regret her past? Her escapades? Her flirting? Her scandals?

She had a slight smile. No, she did not. They'd brought perspective and experiences, taught her about life. Showed her what she wanted and didn't want for herself.

Yet she remained alone, only this time, she wasn't an innocent, and if her couplings with Thomas resulted in a child, life would shift and change once more. Until her menses came or didn't, she waited in a sort of nether world, not able to move forward and no longer able to go backward. If she did fall pregnant, what recourse would she have? Her parents would be devastated, and the gossip would destroy what was left of her father's name and legacy, if any. It would hasten the decline of their health, and by association, the reputations of her younger sisters would be tarnished, stealing away their futures.

It was something she couldn't think about just now lest she open herself up to fresh heartbreak.

One thing was certain, love didn't care what the head wanted. Position and coin no longer mattered. Her heart wanted something—someone—who was unattainable. No number of intentions and good acts mattered. Not according to the Church, that was. And apparently they didn't matter to the vicar, for after her impassioned speech the day the girls went missing, he hadn't come to seek her out.

There was just... nothing. Almost as if what transpired between them never existed.

Another round of tears prickled the backs of her eyelids. How could he not care?

A knock at her door yanked her from her tortured musings. Quickly, she dabbed at the tears with her handkerchief but didn't move from her position. "Come in." She still didn't feel like talking about her time as a governess.

When the door opened, Emmaline came in. As the youngest of all the Hasting sisters, she still possessed a childlike hope in happy endings and a belief in fairy-story magic. In fact, she was around the same age as Miss Partridge.

The woman whom Thomas had already asked to pay his addresses to.

"How are you feeling this afternoon, Gigi?" The cadence of her sister's voice was lovely and pleasing. It was a pity that she'd been so traumatized by the fire that she very rarely left the manor house. "Any better?"

"Not really."

A soft sigh came from her sister. "I'm sorry to hear that." When Emmaline moved around the bed, she perched on the side of the bed near Gigi's feet. "Perhaps you should go outside and breathe the fresh air. Feel the sun on your face. It might lift your spirits."

"I would really rather not, but thank you." The last thing she wanted to find was new hope. "I have enough sun and the breeze here."

"That is not the same." Emmaline peered into Gigi's face and smiled. "If I go outside with you, will you come? Just into the back gardens. Mama said one of the neighbors repaired the fountain recently, so the water is constantly moving now and no longer brackish."

"I'm glad to hear that." The fountain in the gardens had always been one of her favorite places on the estate, but it hadn't worked for years of late, and Papa didn't have the funds to engage a tradesman.

Emmaline nodded. She gathered her long blonde hair, twisted it into a knot, and then secured it with a long hair pin she'd pulled from God only knew where.

Then she frowned. "Wait. Why would you voluntarily leave the house? You have never once wished to do that since you were adopted into the family."

"I know." Her sister ducked her head. A faint blush stained her cheeks. "But if I have a chance to make you feel better, I will do it… even if it frightens me."

The sacrifice tightened Gigi's chest. That was exactly how love should work, making someone happy no matter what. With a gasp, she maneuvered herself into a sitting position. "You would do that for me?"

"Yes." Though there was apprehension in her eyes, Emmaline nodded. "The gardens are supposed to be beautiful right now, and Mama often goes out there to weed and trim when her mind is troubled." She shrugged. "I remember how you enjoyed spending time there."

"Oh, dearest, it's a lovely sentiment, but you don't need to do this for me." Taking in a deep breath, Gigi let is slowly ease out. Again, she glanced out the window. "Perhaps I should visit the gardens. A walk might be just the thing to lift me out of the doldrums."

"You should change into a prettier dress, then."

"Why?" She frowned. "I won't see anyone, and neither will I visit with the neighbors."

"When a lady puts on a pretty dress, she will instantly feel better." So saying, her sister bounded off the bed and moved over to the armoire across the room. When she swung open the doors, she smiled. "You must wear this one. It's so summery and cheerful."

Gigi huffed when her sister held up the garment. Made of a cream silk blend and lined with lace at the bodice, it had a robe-like garment of sky-blue silk, also lined with lace. "I don't remember the last time I wore that." It had been new a couple of years ago before Papa somehow lost all his coin. "Besides, it is a gown, more suitable for dinner or a rout than a walk in one's personal gardens."

"Then it's all the more important to put it on now, else it will be wasted. And it doesn't matter the occasion." Emmaline draped the gown over her arm. "Come. I'll act as your maid and will even help with your hair."

"Such a lot of fuss for nothing." Yet the idea of cleaning herself up and returning to some semblance of normalcy appealed to her.

A half hour later, Gigi had donned the gown. Emmaline had twisted her hair up into a simple but glamorous updo then somehow convinced her to don opera-length gloves. It wasn't necessary, yet she did it to humor her sister.

"Now, lightly pinch your cheeks and bite your lips to encourage the color to circulate." Emmaline smiled. "It simply won't do to have you looking like death. You might cause the flowers to wilt."

"Do stop." Gigi chuckled, but she did it anyway. Then she allowed her sister to link arms with her and they went downstairs and ultimately outside to stroll the paths of the rear gardens, moving slowly toward the small clearing at the center where the fountain rested.

The closer they came, the more she became aware of a ruckus that sounded like the irritated honking of geese as well as childish giggles. "What in the world is that?"

Emmaline's hand trembled on Gigi's arm. "I would have no idea."

Poor thing. No doubt she was terrified they would meet someone by accident, and she would be forced to socialize. Then there was a string of curses mixed with commands in a masculine voice that she recognized, and she gasped. "Thomas." A shiver went down her spine. She glanced at her sister. "You tricked me."

"You wouldn't have come down if I'd said he was here." She dug her fingers into Gigi's arm. "I saw him from one of the windows upstairs and knew instantly he was here to talk with you." She smiled and happiness twinkled in her eyes. "He brought his nieces, so that has to mean something."

Then they reached the clearing. Gigi came to a halt and dug in her heels, refusing to go forward any farther. The soft tinkling of the water in the fountain helped to calm the racing of her heart, but seeing Thomas trying to herd the same pair of geese that lived at the pond into the fountain's pool had her trying without success to stifle her laughter.

"Oh, dear Lord, he even brought a swan." In fact, that regal bird was already floating happily in the pool, yet it was all too evident the bird was far too large for the space.

"It's romantic, don't you think?"

"I…" She didn't have a chance to make up her mind, for the geese chose that moment to spy her, and with honks of recognition, they quick waddled around Thomas and advanced in her direction. "What should I do?"

"Go see what the vicar wants," Emmaline said in a low voice. She gave Gigi a tiny push. "And look at him, Gigi. He's gorgeous." Amusement threaded through her voice. "When he's not clinging to tradition or properness, he's magnificent."

"That he is," she agreed in a barely audible whisper. "But why is he here at all? And with waterfowl?"

Her sister giggled and gave Gigi's shoulder a prod. "Best go talk to him. Perhaps he's examined the depths of his heart and is prepared to offer it to you."

"Oh, dear." Her stomach muscles tightened. "He didn't need to do that." Yet a kernel of hope bloomed in her chest, and with a sigh, she moved slowly toward the fountain even as the two geese met her and provided an escort. Then she only had eyes for the vicar, and she openly peered at him. "Good heavens, he hasn't shaved this morning." The shadow of black whiskers clung to his jaw and chin… and it was one of the most erotic pictures she'd ever seen. Wisps of heat curled through her lower belly. What would that friction feel like against her skin?

Emmaline followed softly behind her. "Perhaps he will propose," she whispered.

Oh, no! A wave of cold panic rose in her chest. "I don't know about that. We are far too different…" Life was constantly in flux and changing, and it terrified her of where she would end up in that mess. "We won't suit."

Wouldn't they? But now… seeing him again, having him here felt… right.

What if I'm wrong?

"At least listen to him. He's so handsome, and that grin!" When Emmaline came into Gigi's line of sight, she winked. "Love isn't supposed to be easy, and shouldn't a man need to show you the depths of his regard with a bit of groveling? And when you are honest with yourself, you love him, so let him have his say. He *is* trying."

"Right." Gigi nodded. She waved to the little girls, who sat with composure and smiles on the lip of the fountain. How had he encouraged them not to run amok? Slowly walked toward Thomas's position while drawing a deep, calming breath into her lungs and letting it ease out in an effort to calm her frantic heartbeat. The soft honks from the geese gave her confidence, and she absently stroked one of the goosey heads. When the swan saw her, it trumpeted, which set off peals of laughter from the girls.

"Hullo, Thomas." Her nerves felt strung too tight while flutters skated through her belly. Indeed, that grin of his made her want to toss everything to the wind and kiss him.

But she wouldn't, at least not in front of the girls.

"Good afternoon, Genevieve." The pleasing timber of his voice awoke butterflies in her belly. "I trust you don't mind that I've paid you a call or that I brought some of your favorite people—"

"And geese!" Penny said as an interruption.

"I like the swan," Lily added. She put a hand into the water in an apparent effort to attract the white bird, who completely ignored her.

"Uh, I don't mind, I suppose." What a ninny she was! Despite their time apart, despite the words they'd each said the last time they'd talked, despite her own doubts and fears, despite his adherence to the things that kept them apart, she wanted this man with a fierceness that prowled her insides and tried to steal her breath.

He raked his gaze up and down her person with all the leisure of a caress, and it made her tremble. "You are quite beautiful today, and the gown only adds to that."

"Thank you. I like that you've left your somber suit behind." Gigi wanted to scream in frustration, for these polite niceties weren't needed, yet as Emmaline had said, he *was* making an effort. The buff-colored breeches hugged his lean legs and the boots had been recently shined. His fine lawn shirt had been topped with an ivory satin waistcoat embroidered with green vines as well as a jacket in blue superfine that made his eyes a clear gray. "What are you doing here, and why have you coerced the waterfowl into this garden?"

From somewhere behind her, Emmaline giggled, and when Gigi glanced over her shoulder, her sister ducked behind a grouping of decorative trees.

"I wished to talk with you, to make a speech, and I didn't think you'd toss me out if I brought the girls and the geese."

"And the swan!" Lily was quick to remind him. Only then did she notice that both girls held flowers in their laps.

"Indeed." The grin he flashed had the power to weaken her knees. "Will you grant me a few minutes of your time?"

"Oh, I…" She pressed a hand to her middle where the need to retch made itself known. "I suppose." A tremble moved down her spine. Would he truly propose?

"Good." When he glanced at the girls, they both nodded vigorously. "Right, then I'll come to it straightaway before my nerve gives out." The vicar dropped to one knee. "When I asked you to be my nieces' governess three weeks ago, I had no idea how much you would change all our lives."

"Well, that is to be expected when I am hardly the proper type. Perhaps it was silly of me to think I would ever be a good fit as a governess."

"Nonsense. In fact, I truly believe more women should be like you."

"Oh?" She could hardly breathe, and she held a gloved hand to her throat.

"And in that time, you have surprised me, you have nurtured

the girls as if they were your own, you have held your own against the gossips, have annoyed me several times, shattered my heart…"

"Ah." Well, that wasn't romantic. Gigi bit her bottom lip as one of the geese sat down in the grass near her feet. "Is that all you would say? When last we spoke, that conversation and what occurred just before it was quite charged."

"Yes." Thomas shook his head. "I mean, no." He blew out a breath and gave her a wry smile. "There is so much more." He took one of her hands in his, and tiny little sensations danced up her arm, but when the other goose took exception to his possession with a loud honk and an aggressive posture, Thomas quickly released her. "It would seem you have made an impression on them as well, and they consider you one of themselves."

Gigi uttered a snort of laughter. Even the girls laughed. "Some geese have impeccably good taste."

"Yes, well, I quite agree on that count. You *are* a remarkable woman." He paused with a frown as if sorting through his speech in his mind.

"While I thank you for that, nothing has truly changed between us, Thomas," she said in a low voice. "I am *not* a suitable woman for you or your life."

"I have given that quite a bit of thought ever since you left. Hell, I've even petitioned God on my knees for more hours than I care to admit, asking Him to help me make sense of the confusion I feel and everything I have experienced since you came into my life."

"And what were you left with?"

"More of the same." He blew out a breath. "So I appealed to the only people I knew had the power to sort me out."

"Who?"

"The girls." He shot them a grin, and they waved back, though she suspected if he didn't get on with it that Lily would tumble accidentally on purpose into the fountain's pool. "They helped me to realize that being a lovely person can come in all forms and manners, and that I would only find stodgy, boring people in the congregation."

Oh, dear. Gigi bit her bottom lip to keep from laughing. Perhaps too much of her had rubbed off on them. "Well, they aren't wrong."

"No, they aren't, and I also took *your* words under advisement while I couldn't sleep these past three nights." Need warred with affection in the stormy gray depths of his eyes.

"I haven't been able to sleep either… because I am continually haunted by memories of you."

"Oh?" The hope on his face left her weak at the knees.

"Yes." She nodded. "But please continue. No doubt the girls are growing restless, and the male goose might rush at you." If he chose to ask her to remain in his life, he would need to do better than that. Too many hurtful words and assumptions on his part had made her feel ashamed of being who she was. "What of Miss Partridge?"

"I told her in no uncertain terms that I wasn't interested, that my heart belongs unequivocally to another."

"It does." It wasn't a question.

"Absolutely, and I no longer have the strength to fight that realization or deny the feelings." Risking the ire of the goose, Thomas renewed his hold on her hand. "Despite myself, despite my position in the Church, I have become overwhelmed by you. I am afraid if I continue this unorthodox and quite scandalous courtship of you, I will eventually lose myself in you—in us—and I will forget my calling quite gleefully because you simply amaze me."

More flutters danced through her lower belly, for those were lovely words indeed. "Yet you said before I wasn't the type of woman you needed by your side."

"I did say that." He nodded and glanced once more at his nieces. Penny urged him to get on with it in a hand gesture while Lily had her slippers off and her skirts hiked up as she waded in the pool. "However, upon further reflection, I was horribly wrong."

"You were?" her hand shook in his. "How so?"

"Goodness and faithfulness come from a person's soul, not by how many times they attend a church service or what current gossip says about them." He tugged on the knot of his cravat with his free hand. "Children and animals are the best judges of someone's character, and you have that in spades, Gigi. I was a nodcock not to see it sooner, and I'm embarrassed that I let pressure from the Church and someone else's dictates lead me on the path away from you."

Her heart trembled. "Thomas—"

"Wait. I am not finished." His Adam's apple bobbed with a hard swallow. "I'm not perfect; I have flaws and am working on conquering."

"So do I," she said as tears filled her eyes. "But don't you think the imperfections are something that will keep the mystery alive? Something we can work on overcoming together?" Assuming he did intend to ask for her hand after all.

"Of course." He nodded. "There will undoubtedly be days where we'll fight and stay cross at one another. But I can also promise you happy days and plenty of blue skies. A lifetime of devotion." His shrug pulled the jacket tight across his chest. "And if this decision means that I'll lose this position, so be it. I shouldn't wish to be the leader of such a judgment filled congregation anyway."

The fact he would put his living in jeopardy for her yet again astounded her. A few tears fell to her cheeks. "I couldn't ask that of you."

"I'm giving the decision freely." The wonderful man brought her hand to his lips and kissed the gloved back. "Ah, Gigi, you humble me. Without prompting, you gave of yourself and supported me. You encourage me with your words and actions, with your caring and nurturing. I want all of that and more with you." When his voice broke, her hand trembled. "Above that, I wish to have the right to give everything that I am to you, for I simply cannot live without you."

"You are not without your own sterling moments, you know," she said quietly. "I adore how protective you are, how diplomatic you have had to be, how you infuse such heartfelt feeling into your sermons, how you care for your nieces, and have never once complained about anything... except my behavior."

Faint ruddy color climbed his neck above his cravat. "I apologize for that. It was the sin of judgment, and I had no right."

"I fear I will fail you, damage everything you've worked toward."

"Then we will work through the difficulties. As a team, and if that riles up some folks, then this isn't the place I need to be." He cleared his throat. "Nothing else matters except that we are together."

Penny let out a loud yawn worthy of a Drury Lane stage. "Get on with it, Uncle Thomas. Ask your question already so we can go swimming."

"Right." When he chuckled, Gigi did too, for the little girl's words broke the tension and centered their emotions. "All of that to arrive at the point. Genevieve Hasting, I love you. Plain and simple, I've thrown my hat over the windmill for you, and I can assure you these feelings go well beyond lust and desire." He winked, because the girls couldn't see him. "I want to expand the connection we share, want to revel in it for the rest of my life, so can you see it in your heart to make me the happiest of men?"

Before she could answer, he cleared his throat, and the girls came running over. Penny put something into his free hand.

He held up a ring made from a daisy and its stem, just like the ones she'd taught the girls how to make days ago. "Will you marry me and be my wife?"

"And be our new mama?" Lily asked with her customary enthusiasm, as she held out a wildflower wreath. "I asked our Mama. She just wants us to be happy, and it made me warm in my belly."

"Oh." Another wave of tears filled her eyes. Was there ever a more romantic, heartfelt speech or proposal? Her hand shook in his as she met his hopeful gaze. "I love you too." She gave into a soft laugh. "I love you girls as well, but I rather hoped I wouldn't turn into a watering pot again. I have been crying since the fete, it seems."

"Such is life, sweeting." Thomas grinned. He tugged on the fingers of her left-hand glove. "Emotions are part of us, and life is sometimes messy. You taught me that."

"Yes, it is." She nodded, and when he had trouble with the glove, she wrenched it from her hand. "I never knew that falling in love would be such an emotional affair, nor that it would be yet another change that has the potential to be terrifying."

"It's understandable, but change is also a part of life. If there wasn't change…"

"… there would be no butterflies." Penny rolled her eyes heavenward. She huffed as she looked at Gigi. "So, will you marry Uncle Thomas? He said your family lives in a big house, and I want to see it."

"I would very much like to marry him, but…" Focusing her attention him once more, she sighed. "I have my own flaws and I'm certainly not perfect."

"You don't need to be. I love you as you are."

She swallowed around the ball of emotions in her throat. "I refuse to be put on a pedestal for you to admire or treat me like a goddess. And I certainly will not mold myself into some sort of dull creature merely because you think that is what a vicar's wife should be. I am my own person who knows her own mind."

"I completely understand, and I've learned that lesson well." His hand holding the daisy ring trembled.

Gigi nodded. "Changing who I am to suit your life would be much like caging one of these geese." For that matter, how the devil had he transported the birds? "I'm not a proper *ton* woman, and never will be, and I suspect I'm not a proper church lady either."

"Which is one of the reasons I adore you." He squeezed her fingers. "I've become accustomed to *you* and the way you've sent *my* life tip over tail. Besides, I would imagine once you're wed, most of your scandalous exploits will come to an end." He winked again. "Remember, I said *most.*"

"Oh, Thomas." Another veil of tears pooled in her eyes. "I'll make mistakes."

"As will I."

"It's how we learn," she added in a barely there whisper.

"Jesus wasn't perfect either, love. He would be appalled to even think that anyone tried to hold themselves to an impossible standard." A sigh escaped him. "I'm learning that also because of you, which makes me wonder why I ever went to seminary." When he once more gave her that specific grin that threatened to turn her insides into mush, she sighed.

After another volley of tears, she had no choice except to blow her nose on the handkerchief he offered. "Pardon me. That's hardly romantic."

"Now that all the preliminaries are out of the way, will you marry me, Genevieve? Life won't be nearly as exciting without you in it."

"Yes, of course I will, and I'll be happy to do so." After he stood and slipped the daisy ring onto her finger, and she took the flower crown from Lily and put it onto her head, Gigi threw herself into his arms. In a low whisper intended only for his ears, she added, "I'm marrying you because I need *you* and everything you are, not because your congregation demanded that you wed. I'll try my best to be everything you want in a wife, but at the end of the day, I need you—the man—and I am only me. Everything else is merely window dressing."

"Those are the best words I've heard in quite a while." Despite Penny and Lily looking on, or perhaps because they were, he gently kissed her. When she curled her hands into his lapels and a surprised moan escaped her, he claimed her lips with more authority that had heated pleasure pinwheeling through her chest.

Oh, she couldn't wait until they shared a bit of privacy!

Eventually, common sense returned. Gigi pushed him slightly away before she became drunk on him. "I look forward to years of discovering the man you truly are behind the image of the vicar."

"Haven't I done enough to show you that already?"

As she laughed, it was as if everyone moved at once. The girls rushed over to hug her while Thomas stood looking on with a shocked expression. The male goose honked and nipped at his buttock while the swan flapped its impressive wings. Behind them, she heard Emmaline's giggle, but when she glanced over her shoulder, her sister had beat a hasty retreat back to the house.

Gigi let all her worries fade as she was held within the knot of her ready-made family, and when Thomas's arms came around her as well, she sighed. No, life wasn't perfect, and neither did it need to be in order to enjoy it. Theirs might be an impossible match, but it was right for them, and it was exciting to think about where they would end up in the future.

As long as they had love in one hand and faith in the other, change wasn't so frightening... and perhaps God already knew that.

EPILOGUE

October 1, 1820
Hawthorn Cottage
Pavenham village
Bedfordshire, England

GIGI COVERED A yawn with a hand. She'd almost fallen asleep right in the middle of tea with her husband. He'd given a lovely sermon that morning, or so she'd heard from Penny, who'd attended services. As a little lady of eleven, she'd turned into a studious child who took great delight in her schoolwork with various tutors, which occurred at Andover Hall, where there was more room, since the vicarage was becoming rather crowded. The girl was also a grandchild after Gigi's mother's heart in that she adored being quite proper.

But then, Gigi wouldn't have it any other way, for the girl was perfect.

As she sipped tea, her mind jogged over how much her life had changed since she'd married Thomas during the Christmas-tide season in 1817. It had made the most sense, for her two oldest sisters were in the country at the time, so all her family had been there to witness the ceremony. Then she'd been delivered of a son who arrived in late March of 1818. He had been conceived, no doubt, during that first coupling she'd had with Thomas when she'd held the ill-fated governess position. He was the very image of his father, and he'd captured her heart the second she'd laid eyes on him. They had named him George after her own father.

Unfortunately, her dear Papa had died in December the following year, and the family grieved the loss. As was the case with an ever-changing life, Gigi's second child had arrived in late March of 1819. A girl, this time, with the dearest little blonde ringlets and big blue eyes whom they'd named Marigold.

This year saw Lily turn nine and she was still a wild hoyden, content to spend most of her time outside, running through the wilderness, and Gigi hadn't the heart to bid her nay. There was much to learn from nature, and she was a little girl yet. There would be plenty of time to learn social graces and a trace of manners; she was, after all, a viscount's granddaughter, but there were other things for her to cultivate than being a society miss.

Society wouldn't have the chance to steal away the girl's personality, not if Gigi had anything to say about it, wife of a vicar be damned.

Throughout it all, Thomas had been a lovely husband, always by her side with support and protection. He doted on his nieces and had fallen absolutely in love with his children. As for his church, well there had been some upheaval after their engagement had been announced. He'd lost a quarter of his flock, for those people took great exception to the match. Perhaps that was just as well. Gossips and people who caused dissent weren't welcome, and if they couldn't accept the fact Gigi would be the vicar's wife, and that she loved the man to the ends of the earth, they needed to find another church.

Eventually, after she wed Thomas, things settled down. Routines were established, and she did her best in acclimating to her new position as well as the fact she would soon be a mother. There was a large learning curve to all of it, and sometimes the girls and her had some friction as everyone had to get along, but by and large, they were a happy family.

Over the months and years, she had come to a new appreciation of the presence of religion and the church in their lives. Occasionally, she reminded Thomas that it wasn't the be-all and end-all of existence, that he had an identity beyond being a vicar, and that usually brought him back to center. Was she as devout as she probably should be? No, she was not, but then that was a personal decision for everyone, and it wasn't up for debate. A person could worship God—or not—on their own terms. She'd taken on many causes and learned to enjoy visiting various people within the community, but hosting monthly teas for the ladies of the village was her favorite thing. It was the closest thing to society she had in the country.

But then, Thomas always managed to surprise her, for twice a year, they took a trip to London to visit his brothers and immerse themselves in the culture and busyness of Town. They hadn't been able to afford a wedding trip, and she couldn't travel in her condition. Besides, it was good to show his nieces the world in which they would be a part of later in their own lives, one which happened well beyond the church. While she adored those times and wearing pretty gowns and attending social functions, each time they returned to their dear little vicarage in the country, she breathed a sigh of relief.

That was much where she belonged, and that had surprised her as well.

Beyond that, she took great pride in tending to her garden, plus she kept chickens and ducks. Some of the eggs they used in the household; the rest she sold to the bakery in the village. The pair of geese had discovered where she lived and were frequent visitors to the vicarage. Every summer they brought their new clutch of babies so she could dote on them.

Never in her life had she envisioned herself in such a domestic situation or that she would adore every day of it.

"Are you well, love?" Thomas asked with amusement in his voice as he set his teacup into its saucer and laid them both on the low table in front of them. That is the third yawn you've had since we sat down."

"I think so." Perhaps it was time to tell him of her suspicions of a dear little dream. "Actually, there is something I must discuss with you." Especially since Penny and Lily had gone over to visit with her mother and Nora and Emmaline, who both spent at least part of the year in the country even though they'd married recently.

"All right." Concern wrinkled his brow. A few strands of gray glimmered at his temples, for being a country vicar was, at times, cause for worry and anxiety. "There is something wrong; I can feel it." He turned to her on the sofa, and when his knee knocked into hers, charged sensation streaked up her leg. "Tell me the truth. Are you well?"

"Yes." She nodded and took one of his hands. "As far as I know, all is well with me." When she peered into his eyes, she thrilled to see the same love and affection she always did. After nearly three years, his affection hadn't dimmed. "Are you content with our life as it is?"

"Of course. Though we have a full house, there is no end of happiness and satisfaction."

"And you love our growing brood?"

"How could I not? Our son and daughter are the most adorable babes I have ever seen. And I never knew how lovely it was to become a father." Again, concern clouded his eyes. "Is there something wrong with one of the children?"

"No! Nothing like that." With her free hand, Gigi cupped his cheek. Oh, he was still so handsome, and she couldn't wait to have him alone with her tonight. "I suspect I am increasing again; I've missed two cycles of my menses."

"Ah, and that is why you've been feeling queasy in the mornings." A slow grin curved his lips. "We will have another baby?"

"Yes, but I haven't been seen by a midwife to confirm my suspicions." A bit of relief twisted down her spine. "In May, I think, but as happy as I am for this, I also think we should take measures to prevent further pregnancies."

"Oh, why?" Truly, he seemed confused about her statement. "The teachings of the Church are adamant that we be fruitful."

She blew out a breath and prayed for patience. "Perhaps the two of us don't need to singlehandedly birth a civilization." The humor in her voice softened the words. "I don't wish to spend the bulk of my life pregnant or bearing children. Nor do I want to put my life or further babies at risk. Just because both of our babes were healthy and their births were relatively flawless, that doesn't mean they all will be." Then she shrugged. "If God doesn't like that, He can talk to me directly."

For long moments, Thomas remained silent. Then he nodded. "I never expected to have children at all, let alone find myself married, and quite frankly, I would like to enjoy time with my wife without constantly having young ones underfoot."

"Thank you."

"I'll do what is necessary in that regard, but where will we put a new child in this house that is already too small as it is?" He heaved a sigh. "My brother gave me that financial gift upon our marriage. We have managed to keep it in the bank without drawing upon it, and I wish to save it for our children's future, but—"

She pressed the fingers of one hand against his lips. "Aren't you the one always telling me that God will provide?" When he nodded, she smiled. "We shall seek out a bigger house that is close to the church. If nothing presents itself, we will figure something out. Perhaps Penny and Lily can stay with my mother for a time."

"No doubt they would enjoy that, and it would make taking lessons easier." He kissed the back of her hand. "There have been no end of surprises and adventures since I met you."

"Do you regret that?" It was a conversation they often had.

"I do not." His eyes darkened as he held her head between his hands. "In fact, I am thankful every day for you because I have no idea what I would have done without such a woman to guide me, support me... love me."

"Perhaps it was fate—"

"Or perhaps God's will—"

She smiled. "No matter what it was, I have never been happier in my life as I have been with you." Then, because she hadn't lost her hunger for her husband, Gigi kissed him, put every ounce of feeling into that one meeting of mouths.

"Even though I love you with all that I am, I still believe you've managed to bewitch me." With a wicked grin that promised delicious things, Thomas stood and tugged her to her feet. "Since Penny and Lily are away and the babes are napping, we seem to have a limited amount of time to ourselves." He waggled his eyebrows. "Would you join me in our nuptial bed?"

"Have I ever bid you nay?" She giggled and then exited the parlor with him in close pursuit. When he was in an amorous mood, nothing else would be accomplished... and she didn't mind it in the least.

"Such a scandalous wife I have." He lightly pinched her arse as they gained the stairs.

Flutters of need danced through her lower belly. "You and I both know that wasn't going to change." And thank goodness for that. She would teach all their children why it was important to believe in oneself and to never worry about the opinions of others.

"Thank God indeed." Once in their bedchamber, he swept her into his arms as he softly closed the door with a foot.

Then she was lost in his kisses, secure in the knowledge that she'd indeed married the man of her dreams, and nothing else mattered. They were doing the best they could, and no one could fault them for that.

For life was infinitely better when surprises—and kisses—waited around every corner. But then, she expected no less from being one of the Hasting sisters.

The End

About the Author

Sandra Sookoo is a *USA Today* bestselling author who firmly believes every person deserves acceptance and a happy ending. Most days you can find her creating scandal and mischief in the Regency-era, serendipity and happenstance in Victorian America or snarky, sweet humor in the contemporary world. Most recently she's moved into infusing her books with mystery and intrigue. Reading is a lot like eating fine chocolates—you can't just have one. Good thing books don't have calories!

When she's not wearing out computer keyboards, Sandra spends time with her real-life Prince Charming in central Indiana where she's been known to goof off and make moments count because the key to life is laughter. A Disney fan since the age of ten, when her soul gets bogged down and her imagination flags, a trip to Walt Disney World is in order. Nothing fuels her dreams more than the land of eternal happy endings, hope and love stories.

Stay in Touch

Sign up for Sandra's bi-monthly newsletter and you'll be given exclusive excerpts, cover reveals before the general public as well as opportunities to enter contests you won't find anywhere else.

Just send an email to sandrasookoo@yahoo.com with SUBSCRIBE in the subject line.

Or follow/friend her on social media:
Facebook: facebook.com/sandra.sookoo
Facebook Author Page: facebook.com/sandrasookooauthor
Pinterest: pinterest.com/sandrasookoo
Instagram: instagram.com/sandrasookoo
BookBub Page: bookbub.com/authors/sandra-sookoo